Lin van Hek is a performance artist. Believing that the written word comes to life when spoken, she has organised and participated in many readings, most recently at the Edinburgh Book Festival. She has spent a large part of the last few years touring with "Difficult Women" and it was during these performances that the characters of *The Ballad of Siddy Church* first came to life. Lin is a winner of the *Age* Short Story of the Year Award.

Other Books

Woman on the Stair
The Hanging Girl
The Slain Lamb Stories

The Ballad
of
Siddy Church

by
Lin van Hek

SPINIFEX

Spinifex Press Pty Ltd
504 Queensberry Street
North Melbourne, Vic. 3051
Australia
spinifex@publishaust.net.au
http://www.publishaust.net.au/~spinifex

First published by Spinifex Press, 1997

Edited by Jo Turner and Janet Mackenzie
Typeset in Sabon and Pepita by Lynne Hamilton
Cover design by Soosie Adshead, The Works
Made and printed in Australia by Australian Print Group

National Library of Australia
Cataloguing-in-Publication Data:
van Hek, Lin, 1944 –.
The Ballad of Siddy Church.

ISBN 1 875559 612

I. Title

A823.3

This publication is assisted by the Australia
Council, the Australian Government's arts funding
and advisory body

*Whence come I and on what wings
that it should take me so long,
humilated and exiled to accept
that I am myself.*

Collette, *The Vagabond*

Contents

I am deeply indebted to Joe Dolcé for his treasured friendship and contributions to this book. The typing of the manuscript and the arduous task of listening to stories repeatedly were carried out with a flamboyant goodwill which inspired and uplifted me.

Thank you to Susan Hawthorne, Renate Klein, Jo Turner, Sue Hardisty, Alison Bicknell, Libby Fullard and Lizz Murphy of Spinifex Press. Thanks to Soosie Adshead (The Works) for the wonderful cover design. My gratitude and love to the women who have shared the rich legacy of stories passed on in the old way. May these tales become the threads that unite us all.

This is a work of fiction influenced by real lives.

"No character in fiction is ever wholly fictitious . . . "
Vita Sackville West to Virginia Woolf

The Poetry of Aunties

My grandmother was a difficult woman, you could not get around it. She was born on three different occasions in three different locations and she said her name was Siddy Church. Late at night, she would sit like a giant curious toad, her heavy-lidded eyes turning with her head, her pupils like magic bullets about to gun down any real conspiracies in the room. Her past was too big and diverse for her to govern; people talked about her shady past. She had relinquished her right to her own story.

Countless individuals in the small town where we lived knew the story of Siddy Church and Joe Flood. I remember my grandfather, Joe: he played the mandolin. He sat out on the great sweeping verandah on the first floor of our hotel at the top of the big hill. This verandah ran around three sides of the building and you could see out over everything in the town. The river at the back beyond the chook pen where the lake Aboriginals camped. The ice factory at the side and the bridge with its suspension curves and creaking timbers. The wide deserted street that came from nowhere. This was where I first knew miracles. The beginning of time.

The town had a story with Siddy Church as its primary object of worship. It involved the long love affair and marriage of Siddy Church and Joe Flood. For those who studied the situation closely, a host of other unknown possibilities could pump up their big alien brains. For no sideshow trickery was ever used to conceal the fact that, at thirty-nine years of age, Siddy Church had fallen in love with a woman old enough to be her mother. If Siddy Church had a husband, she was most certainly a husband to my Auntie Mantel Bonlevi who always called her Sid.

I was a child with many aunties. The hotel was teeming with them. A hotel run by aunties. The cooks, the yardwomen, the cleaning women. I grew up with the poetry of aunties. On summer mornings, they would turn on the hoses and water down the tiles on the hotel's facade. All those women laughing and getting their feet wet. I gasp at the memory of the steam rising from the footpath. The sudden silence as they turn off the water and polish with collected fury the brassware on the entrance doors. Joe Flood played his ukulele on the floor above them. You could hear him tapping his feet on the floorboards. I cannot remember my birth or initiation into the demon knowledge that women could love women. The double marriages of Siddy were two separate and different events. The aunties were content. They stood on the sidewalk, hands on hips, sniffing the air. "Heave ho," they said as they hoisted Joe Flood from his bed and washed his backside. "What's wrong with Grandpa Joe?" I would ask. "Nothing that he can remember," laughed the aunties as they buttoned his crisp shirt. "You really are a ravishing man," said Siddy as she shaved his transparent cheeks. "We love you, Joe Flood," said the aunties a hundred times a day in the middle of everything. He had the place of honour in the kitchen. "He used to be a commie bastard," said Grandma Siddy, watching him play his slippery melodies. The afternoon stretched, the wonders gushing forth. What did Siddy carry in her big black handbag? Rolls of money tied up with handkerchiefs. Definitely! Everyone had seen those. Many had been given one, in troubled times. There was a tiny gun in there, too. She showed it to me, held it up to the light and I stretched my plump fingers up towards it. "She was once a religious woman," the aunties told me, "before those boys died." I already knew from my mother that her brothers had died and these events had changed everything. "I had a crisis with the church," Siddy told me, "but I still like the Marys." When the priest came into the bar, she quoted the scriptures while pouring his beer. He had known her for a long time. "I went to him after my boys died and he told me, 'It's God's Will.' This church of yours suffers from mystic laziness," she told him. He was in favour of co-operation with her, since she was the owner of the only hotel in three hundred miles. This renegade to the faith could diminish his voice considerably. Siddy was continually threatened by law and church for her friendships with the lake people, especially for allowing them into the bar. She would quote for the priest's benefit, "I act with Jesus to give greater privileges to the Gentiles, allowing them into full membership with the receiving of communion." Which everyone knew meant a free drink. When my beautiful mysterious mother, Paddy, came charging at me with her fists, Siddy or the aunties would lift me away, wrap me in their folds. "She has the grand fury in her, your Mum." They would nod their Celtic heads together and put their hands deeper into their trouser pockets. If I had escaped, I would be laughing with them, but sometimes Mum hurt me and it was a deep feeling in my belly that words could never tell about. "I want another Mother," I would cry. Then Grandma Siddy would put some salt in my soup and say something Big: "If you don't get what you want, think of all the things that you don't get, that you don't want!" To Auntie Mantel Bonlevi on her birthday card every year she wrote, "I seek Thee and sure as dawn Thou appearest as perfect light to me." She wanted to change the name of our pub to The Wilderness or The Mountain of Transfiguration. I agreed that these names sounded better than The Club Hotel which had nothing to do with the poetry of aunties.

The Last Days of Rufus

On a hot January day in 1950, I was up on the verandah with Joe Flood high above the hotel. He was
perched neatly on an old hallstand. His still black
hair slicked back from the bony alabaster forehead
made him look brainy. He was wheezing and took
little breaths between trills on his mandolin. There
had been an episode that week involving my grandmother's cat Rufus. This particularly exquisite
creature was dying, dishevelled and huffing in his ele-
gant dialect. The house was suffering. It was known
to the whole drinking public that we were waiting for
the cat, whom Siddy thought of as an incarnation of
an angel, to die. We were told that cats prefer to die
in seclusion. Rufus determined to conceive the project as a public spectacle. His behaviour, vanities, ties
of the heart, despaired of losing their way. When
Mantel put a hot water bottle in her bed, he settled
on the mound. His heat-seeking became obsessive.
He staggered along kitchen sideboards and stretched
out on cakes taken from the oven. During Queen
Elizabeth's South Gippsland tour, one such cake was
prepared. It was to be served after the flag-raising on
the lawn outside our pub. This very splendid cake

was cooling in the manner prescribed. Rufus could not discuss the crisis which was racking him. Siddy could not, in her distracted preparation for the Royal visit, satisfy his hunger for a kindred spirit. He fell into an exhausted sleep and the phantom of death could not have frightened him more than Siddy's shriek when she found him, with no malicious intent, on top of her cake. He groped to find his way off; the soft squishes of sponge stuck to his paws.

He found his way blindly to the bar and sat on the mahogany counter; the customers fondled him. He moaned his sleepy death-rattle. Everyone said "Poor Siddy's cat, Rufus." Finally, the man from the ice factory suggested to Siddy that he take Rufus to a kindly vet in the next town. He sent animals off with miraculous consoling potions that drugged away plague and catastrophe. In the supple rush of death, a pleasurable floating euphoria carried them gently away. Siddy was heartbroken. Finally, she said goodbye to Rufus who drove off with the man from the ice factory.

After the Queen's visit and time and counselling had shadowed her longing, Siddy began to make overtures to other cats. She still inserted whole sentences about Rufus into whatever else she was talking about. When the man from the ice factory came in for his mid-morning, her seraph eyes rested on him. She pulled his beer and held his eye; slanted, slate-coloured eyes. They shared yet another adaptation of the Rufus fable, then went about their separate tasks. She pulling beers, he drinking them. On a hot holiday morning in a small town, when the bar is crowded and the humour is high, if you take a listening breath you will hear whispered on the air all the secrets of the town.

Siddy Church listened and heard the secret . . . Rufus had been thrown into the furnace of the ice factory, alive. Though nervous of the act immediately afterward, time and a few beers loosened the story, "He had driven straight across the lane after he left the pub with Rufus." He reasoned that a quick death in the flames would be just as good as messing around with the bludger vet. He strode with the cat to the iron-gated furnace doors, hooked them open and plunged the cat in. He made casual mottled reference to Rufus's heat-seeking habits. The story became a laconic anecdote told in the colonial way, festooned with squinting eye movements. His mind wanders. Sound-bites reach poisoned ears, fastballs of slow dying words. She waits for more chatter in her listening. He squats there; neurons flare through her skull. He does not notice that people have begun to move away.

I was there. What I saw was that my grandmother was wreaking havoc. Something piteous and imbecilic was contained in the grief that flew about the room. Signals were cycled in such a way as to control the minds of the people. The rage careering through time caused a new communication, a mind-dread. The vibratory hostility could have been used to drive an engine. Timeworn notions of reliable decency surfaced on behalf of Rufus the cat.

7

It was 1950, before our world was addicted to
petroleum, pesticides and pharmacueticals. 1950, in
its frozen state, takes the form of that day for me
when a man was killed running backwards from our
citadel, the awesome shadowy forces of public opinion pyramided against him . . . hit by a two-toned
Holden on the Princes Highway.

Joe Flood's Sleep

Everyone agreed that Siddy Church had done nothing to cause the death of the man from the ice factory. When the police came, they wanted to speak to the man of the house. The dribble was wiped off Joe Flood's chin and he was propped in a corner and spoken to "man to man". Never once did he come out of the sweetplace that he had migrated to, years before. His own personal hearing-loss eliminated any displays of concern or knowledge of the event. The police, typically, acknowledging his complete indifference to the proceedings, thought him a serious man, with no real input into the affair. The aunties said nothing; the house sync, all the way around was "Shshh . . ."

The inhabitants of the house napped. Grandma and Mantel Bonlevi hibernated in their shaded room all week. Out on the veranda, I bounced on the old bedstead springs to the mandolin tunes. The afternoon prepared itself for the lethargic attendance of long hot sunshine which bought many thirsty drinkers into the bar downstairs. I was working on a somersault on my springs and Joe Flood was finger-picking primly on the hallstand.

The evening comes down and Joe Flood cracks his knuckles. We go to bed at the same time. Out of the window, as I fall asleep, I see my name written in clouds of sky-writing. The sun drops in the exhausted hot sky, my lids are pulled shut. I touch the larger life of dream where the wind blows the pages of the day across the great lawn out into the falling darkness. I sleep for a long time, then some deep sad thing wakes me.

I can hear voices. Every light is lit. Caves of shadow. Light globes tremble. Eerie breezes shudder through open windows. My mother is not in bed beside me. Our door is open. I trail my too-long nightgown out into the light. Overhead lights sway. Everything is creaking and knocking and the wallpaper dances and melts into that yellow that my mother calls ochre. It is a word I have newly learned and I see it everywhere. I am not sure if this is real time or dreaming. I cross the river of corridor into the room that is usually locked. Gran and Joe's room is where the money from the bar is kept. It is wide open . . . this fascinating place. The wallpaper has birds and flowers, the ceiling is high and gold with branches of fruit growing over my head. Sometimes on hot afternoons, my Gran comes and lies on the bed and talks to Joe and undoes his braces and I lie between them. No one cleans this room. It is left as it is. The small tables are piled with clutter: papers and saucers of silver coins and hairbrushes full of my grandmother's thick white hair. The mantelpiece spills over with silver-framed photographs of all of us. Handsome Joe Flood, the agitator, in Union flare-ups. Joe Flood in Russia. Holding hands with my mother, Paddy and her long-dead brothers in the old house garden. My favourite picture is of Mantel and Gran and Joe Flood, hand-coloured and radiant in Sydney after the war. My gran has her big black handbag but she has a flowery dress and looks young and beautiful. I have never seen my Gran without her black apron. The first drawing I ever did, told this story, "My gran has a body like an apron." Her hair is pure white, but in this photograph it is black. A copy of this photograph is in Mantel's room down the hall. That room is clean and polished but not as fascinating as this messy place. Here there is a chamber pot under the bed and it is usually brimming with piss, and musical instruments are standing all around.

Joe Flood sits in bed eating his cut apple, and Siddy does the book work under the lamp at the window. After he has fallen asleep, she goes to play cards with my mother and Mantel. I know this from asking questions. An accepted part of my life was that asking questions could cause everything to get bigger, more intriguing but sometimes muddier. I look around the door. Joe Flood is sleeping under the light of the bedside lamp. He is grinning and one arm is hanging down from the bed. I trail down the long passage towards the stairwell. The landing is glowing from the gaping mouth of light coming from downstairs, where some strange business is going on. I hang over the balustrade and look down on the heads of many women playing cards at the old table. The cards go between them and they hold them a while in tiny fans and throw them down. Their voices, hushed and ghostly, float up to me on airborne parachutes of understanding. They are drinking. The ice in their glasses goes clink clink. The whisky decanter comes and goes between them. I can only see the crowns of their heads but I know them all. Mantel is very old and has almost no hair on her crown. She is the one Grandma loves the best. I was told this: "But it is not something to worry about," my Gran said, "since it is only a bit more love and it has to do with need and time and is more like adore." My mother Paddy is quick and deals in a flash. I can hear her halting laughter. Her hair is thick and gleams under the light. They are speaking of me . . . good things but too strange to understand. They are saying good things about Grandpa Joe Flood. I settle in upstairs on the landing, listening to all the good things coming up at me in rays of night sun.

They are making jokes, and peals of rowdy laughter dazzle me on the landing. Mantel's voice is soft and husky. She sings and my grandmother plays the pianola. Sometimes they sing the words on the rolls that go around but other times, they make up their own words. My mum joins in. They return to the card-table, dim the lights and turn a glass upside down. Now they are very quiet. They make no noise and close their eyes and each one puts a finger on the glass in the centre. I am trying not to fall asleep. I stumble back to the bed where Joe Flood is sleeping. I climb into the bed beside him. He is a little man for a grown-up. He doesn't feel much bigger than me and I am not yet seven. I have the feeling that he'll wake up but sleep has me. I am gone with child fatigue.

The morning was old as I came into the kitchen. Women were greasing baking dishes, cutting chicken breasts in half and flouring down oven trays. I had stretched in my bed until cooking fragrances, warm and spicy, seeped through to me. Siddy had her sharp knife and basted a bird. I did not stop to wonder why I had awoken in my own bed. I was never sure of real or dreamtime. My mother was chopping onions, tears rolled down her cheeks. She wiped her eyes on her apron. Sometime in the morning, the aunties tell me that Joe Flood has died in the night but I keep forgetting this. After we had eaten and many people came and went, the day felt particularly different. I went to look for Joe Flood on the hallstand. Siddy was sitting there. She dabs her eyes. I ask her if she adored Grandpa Joe. She said, "No! It was just ordinary long-time knowing," and hastens to add, "this is a different kind of love altogether," and she tells me just because I have learnt a new word, I should not over-use it or wear it out. I ask her, "You mean like ochre?" and she says, "No, I mean like adore," and she starts howling loudly and I am mightily impressed and stroke her face with my grubby fingers. At the funeral, there were many women. Dozens of handsome old ones all singing "The Ballad of Siddy Church and Joe Flood". Some with guileless whirlpool eyes, others with a narrow glint of cunning.

Many trees with gnarled trunks and manicured foliage grew in this glade of the dead. Groups of old women in the trees. The men stood near the cars and kicked the tyres and jangled their keys. Each and every old woman drew her eyes across my face. "Old women always recognise the souls of children," said Siddy Church. I felt very good in the trees with the old women. The rain pelted down even though the sun was out, and marbles of ice fell from the sky and we collected them. All the umbrellas went up and the talking was about good things. It was a very good day. Memorable. Siddy wore a new black wool dress. Mantel wore an ochre jacket and had to be lifted over a puddle by Siddy, who cried and laughed about Grandpa Joe whom, I secretly believed, they really did adore.

Life continues without Joe Flood. Now he is not there, I cast my attention further afield. I venture to the rickety backstairs that my mother sits on to read the *Argus* newspaper. It is here that she cuts my hair in the Chinese style and we eat licorice straps and I get splinters in my legs. My mother does not laugh much but when she does her smile is like mine, toothsome and bursting with that energy of fierce pent-up force that we are. Sometimes I get brave and go right to the bottom of the stairs through the chicken yard and out of the back gate to the path that leads to the river. I walk a short way and walk into the makeshift camp of empty tins and bottles and a forty-gallon drum filled with fire. Here I see the man who comes to drink in the bar. Gran gives him a bird sometimes and other times he takes one. Sometimes when she offers him one he says, "I can't take this one from ya, Mum, because I already took one when ya weren't looking." She tells me that this is an example of his impeccable honesty but says to him, "Oh, I see! Well, I'll eat this one myself then!" And we do. I ask him "Are you an Aboriginal?" And he rolls back on the river bank in silent laughter and his kids make me run very fast dragging me along by my sleeve. I am the smallest and they tie me to trees and I eat dirt if so directed. In great earnestness they tell me: " This is our way." Sometimes they leave me tied to the tree for hours and they go to town and I stay there crying with tears drying on my snotty face. If I don't go to find them, they climb up the plumbing pipes on the back wall of the hotel right up to the second floor. The chooks get upset and Mantel thinks it's a fox and shoots at the imaginary animals through the coalshed window.

Everyone says Mantel is senile now. A word I have learned. I often use sentences with senile, ochre and adore all mixed up together. Miss Cross, my teacher who comes to the hotel to teach me, says I repeat myself. She has plaited rolls on the side of her head and doesn't answer questions. If I ask a question, she tells me: "I'll be the one to ask the questions, Missy."

When I start real school, I play marbles with the twins, Harry and Gil. We draw circles with a stick in the dirt. I spend all my pocket money to buy Gil marbles because he is the one I adore. My Gran says, "You can't buy friendship," when she finds out that I am doing this. I already know this because he doesn't like me at all, not even on Sundays when I am dressed in my claret-coloured velvet with a lace collar, and white socks. I look in the mirror and think it is perhaps because of the rude-looking scab I have down one side of my nose. He has never seen me without this affliction. I fell off the sheltershed roof on the first day of school and cut my nose on an overhang of roofing iron. It hasn't gone away because I keep picking it with my dirty fingers.

A man in wide trousers comes to the school fence. I am sitting in the dust with the marbles. I look up past the expanse of trouser material, the foldings of thick woollen pleats. I look into eyes that are mine and I know, without knowing anything much, that he already knows my name.

"I'm your father."

A shock of hair comes from somewhere across laughing eyes. He sweeps it back and me up and I forget I am almost seven and my knickers are caught between my bum and the twinnies are looking scared because he might be a bad man. We walk the length of the one wide street that is my town and everyone knows who I am walking with and if they don't, I tell them.

I don't remember too many events surrounding my father. My brain is idle when asked to produce character-based information. He came not long after Christmas. My presents were still in evidence. My father made me a cardboard dress. The skirt was in eight parts joined by very fine pieces of copper wire. A flying elephant was painted on its side in silvers and pinks with hyacinths and seagulls and waves, boats, buildings and buses. Cherubim and serpents and moons, stars and planets. The wings and trunk of the elephant came magically off the skirt in three-dimensional splendour. The bodice was covered with intricate suns and trees and faces, rivers and chocolates and dogs holding other dog's tails. My mother said he had painted it all himself and that it was the only thing he was good for.

My father cuts a bright path of pleasure through the house. He teaches me to write my name upside down and to draw Mickey Mouse in one line without lifting the pencil from the paper. He dresses me in my cardboard dress. I can walk into it, like a cupboard. He says I am the "Queen of Make-Believe". That is all I remember. Soon, he is gone. I kept my cardboard dress for many years.

Something was always happening. I came home from school at three, Gran and Mantel would be standing in the saloon bar giving advice to a bruised wife or financial assistance from a knotted handkerchief. They both had a profound preference for anything off-the-books. They took bets, bought and sold anything, swapped and bartered and rolled the off-the-books money into numerous hankies that were slipped into apron pockets or down bodices. This was floating money. It was given away, misplaced, wasted, stashed, or circulated. Money that was alive and doing. Gran's floating money could blitz people's problems, change their circumstances for a week or two. It paid for operations and escapes, sleep-outs for extra kids, chicken coops for the widow's chickens. Giving life-saving advice was Mantel and Siddy's exclusive domain; they were big-ticket players because they backed it up with generous cash-flow and a follow-up fine-tune that made people feel cared for.

These were the times I knew of. The crisp clear picture of motion and detail; smells can refresh my memory, interlace my pictures and generate a photo-realism with no flicker or distortion. Siddy Church with her hair down and the hair nets lying tangled with her arms encircling Mantel. They both have on their pure wool nighties and they rock to and fro to a clean sounding melody that I too can hear. I have been sent from the kitchen with a tray of tea. Mantel has a virus and is acting crazed and will only be still when my Gran consoles her. It has been a long journey from the kitchen with the tray that rattles. The teapot threatens to swamp the Marie biscuits with its boiling amber. They cease to rock and, with glorious hoops of praise, they sweep me into their hollows. We bound into the billowing bedclothes. I can smell the heavy animal scents of their hair all let down and flowing over me. We lie back on the pillows and my Gran tells us a story of the seven dwarves but she changes all the dwarves to girls; Snow White stays just as she is. The dwarf names are a little different; instead of Dopey and Grumpy, there is Fast, Cheap and Nasty, and they are girl dwarves who always act as one.

On this Saturday afternoon, we traipse to the bathroom and run a bath. We are crammed in the tub. The windows are steamed up. Mantel has her glasses on and rubs little circles in their windows. We wash our faces and fannies with the blue facewasher with the tulip border, and towel each other pink, Mantel's goaty tits swinging from side to side. I am rocking with laughter. Talcum powder and wet towels litter the floor. We have trashed the bathroom and it is an issue. My mother Paddy is annoyed and tuts and sighs and crusades with the aunties to shame us.

I was venturing from the hotel more. My world broadened. There were no grown-ups upstairs after Joe Flood died. They were kept busy from four to six in the bar. My grandmother walked the floor at six, saying, "Thank you, ladies and gentlemen, closing time." In those days, if you did not have everyone out dead on six, you could lose your licence. There was a great rush to the bar at five-to-six.

My seventh year was the bravest time in all my life. My mother, by instinct, with no evidence of foul play, had begun to lock the door at the top of the outside stairs. The keys stayed in her apron pocket. It was a cyclone year. I scaled the plumbing pipes with my friends, fostered by them for my speed and codes of easy belief. We travelled with each other down the river to the creek across the bridge. My existence and identity were celebrated in these after-school-hours of exploration. I was no longer the youngest in the group but I was the only white child. There were no Aboriginal children at my school. Distant cousins were always arriving at the camp. The river was full of tins and bottles. Mid-winter, after weeks of incessant rain, I watched with stoic interest the camp being washed out and the camp families being driven to more sheltered ground on the other side of the river. The water level had not covered the bridge and, in a passionate run, I splashed across to search for them. No one saw me dash from the hotel across the highway bridge.

The Great Bloody Flood

When Eadie Wilt was returned to the aunties after the great flood, she was not at all like herself. The aunties ran their fingers through their cropped hair and whispered that life had hit rock bottom. She walked with a stick and everyone was immediately drawn to her to talk quietly about what she had seen and heard. Siddy and Mantel tried to guess at the possibilities. What could happen to a lost seven-year-old child in six weeks?

I now knew that ochre was a very dirty yellow indeed. I could not imagine a time exactly like it. Beyond the bridge, it was another province altogether. When the policemen drove me home, at last, the women were weeping on the steps, every auntie who had ever been to the hotel was there, compelled to weep at my return. They washed my face and changed the dress that I had worn day and night for weeks and hurried away to get the doctor. The policemen crowded into the room hungrily. They questioned me, with dour faces, on the subject of my fast fading recollections. They were anxious to certify me as safe. I did not have, then, the words to tell them of the existing states of lawlessness I had experienced.

They were insisting that I be examined by the doctor to see if I had been interfered with by any of the
dozen people that I had taken shelter with. It was then
that they broke the rules of the house and my grandmother, worn thin from weeping, threw them all out.

It was during the flood that I learned not to trust
local history. I was marooned during those magic
weeks on the other side of the river. My family could
not get to me. I cannot explain exactly how it was during that first night out in the storm. Lightning hit the
trees in the misty, distant hills. Verandahs were lifted
from houses. I traipsed in the mud with a dry box of
matches in my raincoat pocket. It did not occur to
me that death was anything more than family mythology. I waited for each bolt of lightning and laughter
welled inside me as the world flashed and banged and
exploded. Sheets of hail on my hooded head pushed me
forward. As I made my way across the now streaming
hills towards the old caravan park, I heard the crashing
of the bridge. It cracked in many parts and sped off
towards the lakes. A cart attached to four horses was
yanked along with it. I felt my mouth open in childshock. I knelt in the mud; the hard bright triumph of
the sky loomed above me. I ate a handful of raisins.
The horses thrashed out of sight in a fury of twisted
limbs. The river conscientiously returned to the seas in
foaming outrage.

I slept in the caravan park in an empty trailer with
a dry bed, eating raisins in the dark under the covers.
In the morning the caravan's wheels were almost

under water. There were children's clothes, and I changed into a dress I fancied was my size and shape. A small aeroplane was following the river down from where the bridge once was. The winds were high and everything was dark. Ant people trailed around over in the settlement. They could not see me, a speck over here. In the distance, I could make out my grandmother's hotel in the trees, far away on the other side of the river. The wind lifted things from the ground.

It was here that I always stopped, a lazy fatigue took me into its cocoon. I could not construct the weeks after the first few sentences. Finally people took up the lost time and local history nourished the Eadie Wilt disappearance episode.

One thing was clear-cut: I came back changed and I was not belonging so much. Melancholy folded its wings around my childhood.

After some months, the aunties got tired of my stories of the flood. I was celebrated wistfully and I obscurely regarded myself now in the third person, Eadie Wilt. I wrote in my child's way, in a marbled notebook, of not belonging to the earth. I was hard to contain, no one knew whether I was inside or outside now. I loved the rain and I'd lost patience with ordinary life. I'd slept out in the bush in washed-out ruins, in the backs of jeeps and under cars. I was so dirty with mud that when I finally caught up with my friends from the camp, it barely registered who I was and where I came from. I joined the other children and kept up until I grew too tired and crept off to sleep. Once I slept a whole day. The rain kept on. A tent community grew up and strangers gathered. Social difficulties were fierce, fights broke out. I saw men become cruel and senseless. I fantasised the steamy bathroom with Siddy and Mantel and travelled miles inland by foot.

I found Willy Howe in the front seat of her ute wishing she had petrol in the thing. She tried to educate me to the ways. She was to have her seventh child. So far, all her children were girls.

"You've got to watch all the men with the girls," she gestured towards her father and brothers at the fire surrounded by her pack of girl children. I was convinced by her testimony, which carried an overtone of sadistic intention the outcome of which I could not imagine. I was thankful that there were no men in my house. In the meantime, everyone was looking for me. Finally the Irish bloke saw me there, Siddy Church's little Eadie. Siddy was sentimental about him from then on, and it wasn't until later that I remembered him coming to the camp and Willy needling him for the alcohol he had in his car.

The conventional view of my disappearance was pared down to my being with the Aboriginal settlement and their taking care of me. The scale and intensity of the reverence Siddy had for this shadow community had an unmistakable visionary shimmer. Racial themes were beguilingly portrayed by Siddy, who did not consider herself as part of the unhappy white invader. "My grandmother was dragged here in chains," she told anyone willing to listen. "This is not our land."

Where our land was and how we could get back there was often debated in the bar. Wild Celtic oaths and omens surfaced during these stormy pantomimes.

The flood left me with impressions of who I must touch. People could be smeared or highly polished by near identical gymnastics of life. Willy Howe, whom Siddy had often saved, seemed untouched by events. She was wiry and dreamy. She was on probation for trying to steal a baby from a pram outside the bakery. "No! Not the baby," she told me. "It was the pram. I wanted the pram but I had to put the baby somewhere so I carried it to the Salvation Army rotunda and went back for the pram."

Some stories I believed, but others I had not the slightest trust in. Some are true to myself alone. The basic chronology was not in dispute. I came palely out of a hypnotic sleep after the flood, absent, drugged, inert and dream-logged. My mother, spikey and independent, hammered all the nasties out of me and went to Siddy Church with the devastating news that Willy Howe had masturbated a dog, for grog and the Irish bloke's amusement, "in front of Eadie". It came out, that the children had masturbated the dog for nothing but fun. My mother Paddy was beside herself even before she found out that I had broken the bones in my foot while spying on the Irish bastard who asked Willy to fuck the dog for a ten pound note. She got the old bugger's money anyway by distracting him with an hilarious, flamboyant and rowdy pantomime. The fat man, half demon half imbecile, was well satisfied with this lesser entertainment. Willy winked conspiratorially, "Dog and me fooled him plenty, Eadie, and I can teach you all them tricks."

Everyone waited and listened to the weather forecasts on the radio. Mantel filled the tea urn and made pineapple doughnuts and lamingtons. The aunties had a beer.

Storm clouds gathered. I followed my gran around. Down to the chook pen and the vegetable patch, all my connections were being severed. Joe Flood was not there, nor was the camp on the river ever to return.

Siddy said Willy Howe was a noble woman, took her advice on everything and brought her to live in the hotel. Her raffish smile made her a favourite, despite her illicit activities; even the dog came, though Paddy would not let him in the kitchen near the food. Siddy made much of Willy's wisdom and humour; Paddy's batwinged eyebrows arched jealously. Eadie Wilt believed that Willy had magic at her fingertips, the sort that could part waters with a wave of her hand. The personal conflicts that grew between my gran and mother often centred on behaviour that my mother thought was abnormal. "Who's to say it's wrong?" was what Siddy Church always said.

I looked at my mother and, living in a world that to a great extent was make-believe, in a forceful moment of imagination, I said I hated her. I told myself this as I watched her ferocious raven's head darting from task to task. As time echoed down this particular chamber, I always saw her familiar shape in the doorway, heaving at me in the darkness. I saw her face dark and glowing with its one great gull brow stretching the width of her tormented face, drenching me with fear.

It was in this seventh year that I noticed her, really. Her silence and mountainous sorrow roamed around me and went deep into my soft places and seared my sweet edges.

Sometimes when I was out on the verandah looking at the sky and the movement and formations of clouds, a great parting would take place. I would see my mother in that opening, dark and shadowed and very angry. When I grew to be almost a woman, I wrote in my diary that being her daughter was the ultimate mind-fuck, but even then she could still make me sob openly.

Tears rolled down my face twenty years later when I thought of her dark brilliance. The subtle complex composition of love and a raw pain that I later learned was the pain of many women.

I was a small girl with my hair cut in the Chinese style and my father said I had eyes like moist olives. Of course, I wanted eyes like cornflowers but when the carload of country coppers came to retrieve me from the settlement with the hovels made out of petrol drums, I told them I was seven, four-feet tall with moist olive eyes, and my name was Eadie Wilt. That was after the flood, and Mum and I sat out on the landing on the wooden steps. She cuts my hair in the Chinese style and we eat licorice straps.

My grandmother liked to kneel in the dirt, growing things, "It's healthy," she told me as we lay against the rear wall of our garden, soaked in sunlight waiting for a miracle. "The promises of fantasy are filled with greater splendour by reality itself." I asked her, "Why do you believe that and does Mum believe that too?" This believing was too much of an issue to explain, said Siddy. I wanted to know in my child's way if it was a free choice or something that was forced upon you. My grandmother, I noticed, was sobering up from this conversation. She understood the functions of conserving, patching and mending. She could not tell me why my mother sometimes picked me up by my hair.

A great deal of drinking was done in our house after Joe Flood died. My grandmother was a gentle drunk. She liked to sing in her deep velvety contralto's voice. I surrendered to an ecstatic and reliable excitement when she sang her rapturous songs.

After my lost weeks, my mother was transformed. I hardly knew her. Some catastrophe held her in its spell.

My mother told me she had been taken out of school to look after her sister and her brothers. Always the older sister, keeper of the children. The children in her keep had met with early deaths. When I disappeared, it must have seized her as part of the same evil spell. On the day I came back with misted hair, my blood, bones and arteries safe beneath my trembling flesh, she gave me an uncertain caress, her downy cheeks rubbing mine.

The brothers of my mother weren't mentioned very much. She looked haunted if a name was merely spoken. After the flood were terrible times. During these months, I was introduced to past things. My darling grandmother wooed me with endless stories of family history. Trustee to the repertoire, she passed it down to me. We often met in the quiet dusk at the back wall in the garden. She told me of her love for doe-eyed Mantel, and other years before my coming. By the end of that eventful year, we would pile into the Packard and say goodbye to this town forever. At first, my mother's drinking came painfully. She refused to drink and recoiled from drinkers. Paddy was a worrier. Grandma Siddy said she looked like a Mexican sharecropper's bride. Some days she looked like Hedy Lamarr. I heard her cry morbid tears under the stars. "Those are my brothers," she told me in explanation. Her finger traced two small points in the constellation. My mother's mysterious disposition of the heart intensified after she began to drink. Her esoteric practices opened and closed around me. Sometimes she would come to my bed in the middle of the night. All lights would blaze and she would yank me from the bed. I only touched her twice more in my whole life. When I was eleven, she got sick and couldn't move. She was in bed and she called to me, we were alone. I was repelled and confounded by my fears of her. She told me to help her to sit up and I put my arms around her shoulders. I bit into my lip at her tenderness. The soft melting of her flesh, her shoulders creamy smooth. Her eyes watered in pain. Great welts of love rose across my face, a physical reaction, a rash of love never experienced. She was so small I lifted her in my eleven-year-old arms and carried her to the armchair. In time, she got better and gained control and scared the piss out of me again. Hitting me with her fists and beating me with a coat hanger until three months before my thirteenth birthday when I strode purposefully to the phone and ordered a taxi truck to come to the house to collect my things. "A regular little miss," she screamed and ran at me. I stood firm and she bounced off me like a crushed canary hitting a wall.

Interpreted from any conventional point of view, our leaving the town where I spent my first seven years was irrational. In dreams, things happen which do not happen in real life.

After the flood, the town began a rebuilding program and the land directly next to the pub was sold. It was announced that a building was going up slap-bang against the eastern wall of the hotel, the only side that did not have a verandah. Since the hotel was built on the boundary of the land Siddy owned, our new neighbour had the right to build on his boundary also. He ignored the fact that the hotel had windows down the eastern side and, after a short intense time of argument, the building was erected. There was a narrow space now between the two buildings about a foot wide. The rooms on that side now became gloomily damp, never having the sun and breeze through them. People wondered why Siddy had not protested. She was spending a lot of time in her room where she did the books. Mantel said, "She's gone to the City of Thought," and blithely stoked the kitchen fire that cast rosy reflections across her face. When Siddy came down, Mantel gave her a throttling embrace, the dribble of afternoon tea still on her chin. They were still relentlessly romantic, and Mantel writhing under her kinky coiffure hissed out her sweetest lovesong from a strangled throat.

They went swimming in the ocean one day, taking their Eadie Wilt with them. They drove some miles and parked at a deserted white beach where a wounded lizard rolled in death. It died in the noon sun and Siddy dug a pit and crossed two sticks and then we ran squealing down to the surf. We dived in and out, and Mantel was grinding her teeth with the cold. Siddy was a superhuman swimmer, divine and adolescent in the water. A power plant of energy and optimism. We lay throbbing in the sun, the crusty salt drying on our legs. We shared an affectionate siesta and woke to burning thighs. Walking for miles along the beach in a once-upon-a-time hum of lost afternoon, we believed in a higher charitable justice. We returned home with sea shells at twilight in our mouse-car. Mantel had forgotten rheumatics. She leapt from the car and ran through the lobby with its enchanting lounges. She trailed sand through the corridors, skipping up the stairs and into the vault that was her room on the eastern side with the windows that opened onto the newly erected brick wall.

She jumped agilely onto the bed and reached for the blind to cast out the view of bricks. As she did so, she took a little jump on the inner springs and went straight through the window – at least this was what was reconstructed later. The death throes of Mantel were something that Eadie Wilt was not allowed to hear. I could hear my Grandmother Siddy calling down into the deep crevice between the two buildings. Streams of workers came and tried to get her out but she was stuck there, half-way down with her arms broken. Siddy rocked, with medieval echoes coming up at her from the dark slither of space, in the blackness. Finally, they broke through the new brick wall and carried her out to be buried. It took them six hours and Mantel's nerves had stopped tingling in her fingertips by then.

The aunties gathered in the bar in their slacks and elastic-sided boots. The groaning churchbells infiltrated the room, but Siddy had long ago forgotten the Lord who walked on water and stilled storms with a word.

"Joe Flood and Mantel are dead and Paddy's gone right round the twist," moaned the aunties. If all this wasn't enough, Siddy announced out of the blue that she would marry a certain truckdriver. The hullabaloo brought life at the pub to a standstill. "Sorrow plays a funny fiddle," said Siddy. His name was Norman and he soon convinced them of his virtues. He took his place politely and Eadie liked him. "He is a truckdriver," said Siddy, "but God had not meant him to be one." By the time their heads touched the pillow that night, they were married. A host of merrymakers came pushing into the bar and things began to look up. A few months later, however, we left that town, the whole pack of us. The night before we left, I heard all the stories of what had gone before. My grandmother played all the songs that had ever been sung in that place. We played cards, and Siddy told me how she met Mantel and other things. My mother after midnight was relaxed and radiant and spoke of her brothers. I never knew what was what, but I had the impression that pleasure for my mother was safety and since nothing was ever truly safe, no pleasure was possible. Her voice grew low when she told of her favourite brother, Nip, after she had taken him from the river.

"He looked at me with a reproachful look and did not say another word, his eyes were the strangest yellow colour." "Like ochre," I intoned. They both ignored me as if I was not there. I remembered all those yarns and I could picture everything that happened back then in 1939.

1939 . . . Siddy's Yarn:
"If you can't remember what happened," she told me, "make it up."

Siddy watched Joe Flood on the dunny, that day in 1939. Elbows on his knees, with his pants around his ankles. The can sat over a shallow hole in the orchard under a peach tree. Fruit bats swooped down and competed for the fruit. Later, after he'd gone, Siddy could still see his ghostly form out there. He said he was coming back. She didn't do anything different. She wasn't one to go depending on anyone, especially a soft dear thing like him.

The day was teaming with activity. The river was thrashing madly by. A cyclone up north had triggered another flood. The river crossings were impassable for a few weeks. Joe Flood had cabin fever on the third day of rain. She knew that, as soon as the river was low enough, he'd be off.

His leaving was to him a secret act. There were signs, she thought, invisible to him that showed his bad timing. This day was roaring with summer. It lost no time finding its feet after so much thunder and colliding cloud. The creek spewed its dirty kerosene waters down the mountain to the river. Things were sprouting and shaking and popping quite outside the restraints of reason. Flocks of cockatoos arrived.

Crawking, cracking-seed sounds punctuated the incessant cicadas going strongly berserk. The clearest day, trembling with promise.

When Siddy Church looked back, she estimated that this was a day that she would remember; the fragile miracle of their living trickled and sparkled and later, from the great distance, she felt the charge of that distant day. She threw open the heavy doors and lifted the stale bedding out onto the grass; the scent of eucalyptus sweetened the air. He rubbed up against her leanly, his transparent face sultry and his smile sensual. He had periodic attacks of maleness but mostly he stayed in his own perverse androgynous place, feeling too soft and full of indulgent goodwill to threaten her with any histrionic familiarity.

The kids were down around the creek in the rocks; their whispered shouts carried way up the valley, and bounced against the cliff face into the hollows of trees. Wallabies on the edge of the State Forest sat up and turned their heads to one side, snaffed and scratched and cleaned their paws. The whole screaming activity of the day and the tyranny of the sun and the river drove him on his way. He waved as he walked down the track.

Children's laughter floated up through the brimey pollen-filled morning, the mist rose with mercurial force, coiled and twisted around the hills. Momentous and streaked with sky, the sun scorched with total dedication. Thrilling breezes spiralled down in shafts of clear mountain breath. Leaves leapt about and branches swayed and cracked and thumped to earth. Clouds gathered and quickly promenaded to the edge of seeing.

Siddy made a yellow loaf with coarse floury crust and all of them ate thick greedy slices. All except Joe Flood who was gone by this time. She was sorry he missed it. This perfect brilliant day in the middle of everything. They ate the hot bread. She drifted, bedazzled by life's colours and smells. The day climbed about her; cradled and fondled her. She was never one to save up. They finished off the whole bloody loaf. She laughed at the indulgence.

The copper was back on its rocks on the mound above the river. The river ran frantically along. She bucketed water and collected twigs. She rattled the kids into action. Soon the water boiled. She washed everything in her enchanted reach. The sun shone pure gold.

She had a bag full of washing to do for Charlie up the mountain. Charlie and Mantel were her neighbours. They paid Siddy to walk down the river, collect their dirty washing and return it clean. Charlie also gave her milk and eggs. Today's loaf owed its yellow blush to the outlandish yolks of Charlie's grain-fed chickens. Siddy knew that not too many chooks were grain-fed in 1939.

"Mantel has had it," Charlie told Siddy, "hardly gets out of bed these days." Siddy had grown fond of Mantel, she cleaned her house and made a friend. This day she had misgivings about leaving the boys with Paddy. Joe Flood had just gone and Nip always played up when his dad went off.

Siddy liked this walk. When Joe was home, he looked after the kids. Oh well, it's Paddy now. She trusted Paddy more than she trusted herself. She hauled the washing out into the old tin tub on the end of a long stick. She bucketed water on to it from the creek. The wringer had come loose from its moorings during the flood so she called for the hammer and got it sturdy again. The boys hovered around, looking strong. She called them braves. "I don't think this job deserves the attendance of the braves." Paddy laughed. Happy to be party to this hearty notion that connected her to her mother. One of the tiny revenges. It occurred to Siddy that she wasn't the mother for boys. Girls were faster, they knew what you had in mind, what you were thinking about. You didn't have to spell it out.

Still, the minute she was meanthinking, she was cuddling and nuzzling those boys around. They breathed into her silky black head and thrashed away from her. Slithering into the river, naked skinny eel creatures. They could go across the river underwater without coming up for breath. When they did that she tossed her Celtic head. She was taken forever by that breathless moment when they were out of sight under the water. It marked her. When they came up gasping, she always looked directly at the sky. Thanking someone.

With a powerful pull of her tight slender arms, she

lifted the sheets and undies high into the trees pegged to their rope. A billowing canopy of linen showered above her. Twinges in her belly and bum as she held them high and hitched the rope and knotted it with determined strong fingers. Under the trees, she relieved the discomfort in her bladder. The speeded-up metronome of her cells and arteries made her heart quicken. Though she came to live a different life, she would always be there under the trees with the sweet scent of abandon and heat in the air.

An hour later, the washing was dry and folded tight as a drum. A solid lump of ancient apparel, sheets and nighties. She got it back to white, the stains of snot and piss from Charlie and Mantel were gone. Now they smelled of sky and wind.

She told the kids, "No play with fire or blades." This was the general rule. There were snakes everywhere and a resident brown in the garden. In 1939, Siddy put a lot of reliance on God and luck. She felt that it was a bit vulgar but it had won her over in a subtle religious way. How could she know that, on this very day, her beliefs and trust would fail, leaving her frail and godless.

She washed her face. Her nose shone with authority, brick-red. She knew how to pull herself together. While she did this, her son Nip watched her. She tied laces on her walking shoes. He took notice of how her eyebrows met in the middle of her nose like a flying seagull. He knew all about her. Where was his father, by the way? He liked his father. His father could pick up snakes by the head. There was a special way! Not everyone could do it . . . his father had done it to the brown snake in the garden and it didn't even get pissed off. You had to press in the right places and you could learn it. The gull across his mother's eyes flapped. "Nip! Did you bring all that wood up from the river?" He rattled off with his billycart of logs, applegums and sheoak and a bit of redgum. He looked back at her a look she would remember. She shucked up creek. Solid and heavy, her feet hit the ground . . . shuck . . . shuck. The bundle of washing was heavy. The heavens swirled, the cicadas' deafening clattering came in waves. Across the river, a fat wombat bulldozed along, his thick body steamrolling the grass. It made her feel good to watch the old headbutter belting along.

She wondered how far he had got, what he had smelled, seen, touched with hand and eye, since this morning. He was at that very moment on a bus. He had read the latest papers: Menzies was selling pig-iron to the Japs. He scanned the pages for all the news, the disasters and epidemics of a world in bits.

He wrote her a letter on the bus with the date and time. "Geniuses do this," she told the kids. He missed them already eight hours away. When he took her to this old house, he said that he wasn't sorry that it had come to this. They had nothing and would most probably continue to have nothing.

People in town told Siddy Church that Joe Flood was a genius. She waited for a sign that would show her this. It wasn't until after she had married him that this information was passed on to her. He married her because she was down to earth or something of that nature. The perils and fortunes of their life were malignant enough to have caused several major changes over the years. Alcohol made it impossible for Joe to use his genius in any practical sense relating to their economy. He was a card-holding communist. Communism, thought Siddy, could serve as the name for a malady whose first symptom was the incapacity to get a job.

Joe Flood did not like it if it looked as if she was getting intelligent. If he had been a bruiser, he would have hit her, but as it was they shared an indefinable dependable laughter suggesting maniacs and psychopaths. They did the appropriate things, like have babies, clothe, feed and love them. They lived in rooms and held meetings where the men would bang their fists on the table and spit into the fire.

"Everybody loves bloody Hitler," he was reading the paper, "because Hitler will wipe out communism." She had just got back from the factory. "Joe Flood," she said, "there's nothing for dinner and I've been laid off."

They moved for the third time in six months.

She was a gorgeous woman. People said it, sometimes under their breath. She was reputed to be simple. Common sense dictated that no one bothered to flatter her. Everyone still called her Siddy Church even after she married.

He would play with strands of her hair, roll it in and out of his fingers. He liked the simple company of her, the bold outlook. Her gorgeousness was all bound up with something, he suspected, might well be verging on mental dullness.

Coming out there was the last chance in a series of last chances. They ran from a mountain of debt, eviction and an agenda of intellectual hyperbole that had brought his earning ambitions to a grinding halt. An unmistakable current of happiness ran through Siddy and the children when they were told they could use the old house. Though hardly a house it was. Certainly a room and uneven stone floor and walls, a stone fireplace, and one room with a little room within that large room.

"There's no running water," Joe Flood said forlornly, looking for a tap.

"What do you call that?" She gestured toward the creek. It was visible from the tussocked hump that would soon be her garden.

Gentle Joe Flood, they called him in town. Gentle Joe took the buckets to the creek and filled them. He had been shot at in Union brawls and made harrowing speeches that helped minor reforms, and his mates told her between clenched teeth that he was a bloody genius. For the time being, however, not ever remembering a time when they had anything, she was going to make something out of everything.

So she walked with her own set of principles, all the good times having not been used up yet. Inhaling

her own well-being, she headed for the old goldmine.
The hole was fifteen feet deep with passages going off
into the mountain. She had climbed down with the
kids and taken home discarded picks and shovels.
Today she peered down and jumped slightly: a gigan-
tic goanna, bigger than the one up at the house that
was longer than her broom. It had its front end
embedded noisily in the bum of a decomposing wombat. Old dead vocabulary involving real emotion,
short words of primal candour, sprang from her.
Fright and disgust at the very nature of it. It looked at
her, straining back its head, covered in gunk up to the
eyeballs. Suddenly, this six-mile walk was a discomfort. She decided there and then to change her life.
Her racketeering days were ahead of her. She still was
in that momentary illusion of days unravelling. Her
husband, Joe Flood, roamed unconnected. The children, austere and wild and knowing, ran at the
derelict house, playing with blades and fire and lifting
snakes by the head. She ran in order not to suffocate.
A great frolicking flock of green and red parrots
swooped past her head. She stopped, panting and
threw the bundle down. At this place, she always
rested. She felt the erosion of herself, the annihila-
tion, the complexities of the mountain ridges and the
erotically charged water. The river hurtled downhill,
carrying trunks of trees. They looked like people she
had known. All in passion were dying and screeching
and demanding breath and possession. The sun in its
big hot isolated body stayed fat while the muscles of

the sky gripped it tighter, harder, firmer and it pushed heat out compulsively, obscurely, a violent primitive urge. For no reason, she wanted to cry but she kept walking. No time for bloody tears.

She passed through old homestead sites. From the old orchard, she salvaged some fruit. The cockatoos lifted out of the trees, hysterical wings battering the fruit. In the river, she washed a handful for Charlie and Mantel. With her penknife, she cut a piece and ate it. As she was savouring the fruit, feeling half-good again, something triggered thoughts of her old father. She could feel the grace seep out of her. Disappointment carved up her cheeks. He was her secret. There was nobility in those old photographs of him, his lowered head with his hat perched provocatively, the broad sumptuous trouser legs covering the boney knees that she knew so well. The fabric billowed around him and the mystery of all that material surrounding her father was the first joy she could remember.

She went everywhere with him. Mother's drowsy complacency allowed him to smuggle her out and he fed her beer from the baby's bottle until she was four and life got seriously ugly. A licentious and flowery drunk most of the time, he stole profits from the grog sold at referendum parties and his sympathisers agreed under the loquat tree that there was nothing as dangerous as a silent woman. Father's bashing mother senseless caused Siddy to think in detail about liberty. The vulgar emergencies of their life, a delicate typography etched in Siddy Church's private volume of events that she carried in her head. It fell to her to feed him soup. She saw that his teeth were loosened and she loved him with a galloping confounded hate. While he was recuperating from having bashed his wife, he asked how mother's psychological bruises were. These were uncertain times.

"I am your father, we are of the same rock," he told her. His own bedroom door locked, he thumped down the long passageway and meddled with his daughter. He picked Siddy up like a feather pillow and Mother came running sacrificing herself. He greeted her with a taciturn smile, waving his thing at her and urinating in the passage against her sideboard. Having gained access to his own bedroom, he quieted down. It was his right after all. Next day, he laughed about it and his mates spread the word till it was reduced to: ". . . and then, he pissed on the bloody sideboard," and everyone thought him a real card.

Siddy Church often dreamed of these games. Silly games, her mother called them. Before her father passed peacefully away in his sleep, the cord of enthusiasm for him had grown thin from wear and tear. He died smiling. She shared with her mother a cantering nausea and they both choked on moans of relief. Everyone toasted him and fingered his tattoos at the funeral. Siddy knew how he squatted down on the embankments perving at the kids from the convent. She had a strained clinging memory of being under a bridge with a long-forgotten neighbour's child, a neglected kid who didn't belong anywhere. It was camouflaged, but he was holding her on his knee under a blanket. He was transformed, his head thrown back and flushed. The child's smallness, in memory, her face cringing and hollow and hungry. Siddy had seriously thought about killing her father.

Charlie and his wife, Mantel, laughed like kids when they saw Siddy. He ferreted around with some smeared cups. Burns on his arms and a half-burnt sheet told Siddy that he had fallen asleep smoking. Siddy untied the dog from the bed leg.

Mantel was looking as undernourished as ever, and Siddy chopped potatoes and onions, a quick soup. She got Charlie to kill a bird and plucked and chopped. Mantel talked to her through the open door, twisting in the bed, crabbing and scratching at her idyllic mane with a teenage giggle in her throat. She was like a gentle sea animal, an urchin with her grey and rust-coloured halo. Siddy took her in her lap and helped her. She washed her and drew on her fresh laundered nightgown. She hoped an ancient knowledge might flow through to her from Mantel. Wise her up. Who ever said old women smell, she thought, breathing in Mantel's baby fragrance, marvelling at the smooth unblemished skin on her skinny white haunches that had never seen the sun. Charlie, wise to the world, suspected witchery when he saw this strange sight: Siddy, holding his Mantel in a foetal position in her lap with Mantel's hair foaming all over the place.

"What's up?" he asked. Siddy gently sat Mantel in the chair by the window. A small ray of sunshine touched her. She spread her toes. A smile led to nothing in this life, she told Siddy, and beamed at the strong gravy and weak tea. With a last minute gluttony, she ate the remaining potato. A face so little used to smiling, now smiled while the dishes were washing, the kitchen scoured and the beds stripped and remade with a nurse's precision.

In the months that Siddy had been coming here, she had told many things to Mantel. She knew that Mantel had once loved to ride her bicycle around the hills. The old Packard had got a bit much for her to handle and Charlie's licence had expired, so they parked it in the shed and closed the doors.

Siddy surprised herself by speaking readily of her disappointing father and lovingly about the highbred courtesy of her mother.

Charlie and Mantel were brother and sister. "Now that's something you didn't know, eh?" cackled Mantel, devoutly loyal to the moment of confidence. Siddy was shocked. It's true. She admitted as much. They confessed on and on through the months fine human warmth. The occcasional external phenomenon of Charlie, the husband-brother, joined in and they all felt a sense of being fully alive.

Siddy ran home, the moon guided her. This day of promise was ended. She would never transcend the terror of the night that followed. The house was in darkness, no fire had been lit. She knew that something was very wrong. She moved through the fragrant night, trees charred by the moon, stretching her arms to heaven calling, "Nip! Paddy!" An impenetrable haze, a dark green sea and the chill, the treason of the night. The trees tore at her. She couldn't breathe. She covered an endless expanse of forest. No one answered. Shadows ran along the water. Her heart attacked her, a terrible beating, a nightmare pounding. And then she saw them. Shadows only. Barely moving. She screamed towards them, her lungs burning. Swooping down, circling the river, she was counting them, forgiving them, these wanderers, these flowers, the eyes were on her. Paddy held her little sister, Beryl, and the youngest boy came towards Siddy. "Nip," she said, when she saw him lying there. Her voice soared over the pockmarked hills. She could just make out his peaceful brow in the darkness. And around his head, the bloody swirl.

Cheek-to-Cheek at Mantel's Cafe

Change came. Just after Nip died, a whopping great fire swept over the country. This was the truly transcendental calamity that this suspicious commmunity had waited for. They named it Black Sunday, for it only took one day to burn up just about everything. Songs were sung about it.

The British Prime Minister was promising peace in our time and Germany's Chancellor promised, by infallible means, a pure blood fatherland.

Joe Flood had continued to come and go from the old house. Rustic politics and a folklore marriage mingled superstitiously in the tricky terrain of his intellect. Siddy's imaginative life stood still for a long time after Nip died.

Charlie died in the fire. Mantel, finding him gasping from smoke exhaustion, had dragged him to the shed and got him in the Packard. Somehow, she started the car and had driven it out of the range of the fire. They were both found next day by the firefighters and transported to hospital. Mantel had not driven for fifteen years and she had barely been out of bed for almost as long. Later she described a period of conflict where she threw off the idea of dying and decided to start a new life.

The new life began for Mantel after she moved in with Siddy Church. They watched all the sunsets and dawns and Mantel became eloquent with grace. She said she was throbbing with light. Siddy said Mantel was a scientific curiosity just off her deathbed and so new-looking.

Once Siddy Church and Mantel Bonlevi decided to love each other, they went at it and did not stop. Siddy said, "With conscious wish everything comes." Mantel got younger and younger until she was the same age as Siddy and then she stopped. She drove the cavernous old car with its desperate engine all around the mountain. Her Astrakhan coat buckled around her and her hat rakishly tilted. She had saved all of Charlie's whisky from the fire and she brought it all with her as a sort of dowry.

When Joe Flood came for one of his visits, he looked at these marvellous women. He had travelled all around the world and knew many languages. "Putting them all together I should be able to make this out," he thought. But he could not. He wrote some papers, licking the point of his pencil, then went unhurriedly on his way. Siddy thought he seemed less lucid, a compulsion to beat about the bush, or had this new love modified her man-view?

His next visits were more disturbing however: he had forgotten things. He forgot that he was handsome, romantic, world-weary Joe Flood. He had forgotten Russian and comrades and history but he still remembered Siddy. He crawled into her arms and slept. Mantel made way for him, she knew need, respected it as a major force. On his last coming he forgot that he always had to go. And so he stayed, forgetting something more every day. Siddy and Mantel remembered for him. In all their moves and travels from then on, he came too. He sometimes forgot to tie his shoelaces and go to the toilet. Towards the end, he forgot Siddy and Mantel but that was years away. Siddy knew the name of his malady but always referred to it as his forgetting.

On a blustering evening, both feeling that their life had new meaning, Siddy and Mantel decided on action. Their imaginations were oiling up images of purpose. They packed all their belongings, put on their best boots and slacks and, though petrol was scarce and war declared, they set off brazenly for new horizons.

They took with them five dozen eggs rubbed with fat. Joe Flood and the children enjoyed the scenery and grew irritable in the back seat. All the bottles of whisky were in the boot. A hessian bag of newly dug potatoes was in the front seat with Siddy and Mantel and an assortment of small bags and boxes of toys and treasures and underwear.

Within a month, having travelled widely without any mishap, they began to feel the tyranny of travel. No sooner had they noticed this than a suitable abandoned beachfront shop not far from Sydney aroused their interest. They settled here contently and when they got tired of eating potatoes and eggs, Siddy caught the bus into the city and sold a bottle of whisky to an American soldier. She was shocked at the money he offered her.

Joe Flood mended chairs and proved to be good at it. Mantel sat in the glass window looking out to sea and read the newspaper headlines, "War Bride Makes Good – By Being Bad". Women ruled Sydney then. The sly grog queens stood up to any violence but spent a lot of time in hospital having bullets extracted and razor slashes sewn up. Siddy and Mantel were noticed by the bordello queens and labelled dykes. The rigours of name-calling did not outweigh the exquisite coming-out of Sid and Mantel. If anyone called Siddy Church a bloody dyke, she would comment, "Never use two words when one is sufficient." In the beginning, she said, the names came out like tropical ulcers. Siddy was in the Paradise Zone with her guardian angel. Mantel said, "The reign of Light is at hand." There were coupons for food, petrol and clothing. They were told when to cover the windows and turn off the lights.

The Women's Land Army came in droves on weekends-off and brought with them loads of vegetables. They were toiling the soil for their country. The men were gone and the women danced cheek-to-cheek and made jokes about their need to make do with less. Austerity was the thing. The government even began a programme. Clothes had no buttons or pockets and skirts got very short. So did sheets. Siddy said

you could barely cover yourself with either. She went
out and bought an austerity car that ran on charcoal.
Bad jokes flourished. "Have you heard about the austerity knickers? One Yank and they're off!" Siddy
sold whisky on the black market and set up her cafe
on the beach front. All manner of business was con-
ducted here and Siddy's black bag got bigger. The
Americans never spent two bob when they could
spend two quid and they knew not to ask Siddy if she
had a sister. They knew she had plenty. And they
knew they weren't for them.

One day an American woman who lived in Sydney
donated a Wurlitzer 1015 jukebox. She was part of
the dyke sorority but Siddy said she was a two-sided
coin. The front of the machine was one unbroken
arch of moving light. Bubbles rose from four invisible
sources at the base and converged at the top of the
full arch while multi-coloured fluorescent tubes
revolved slowly within the two pillars. The jukebox
and immediate surroundings were bathed in the soft
warm glow. Dancing couples, mostly women, filled
the glass-paned windows of the shop that looked out
to sea. Mantel was an exceptional figure silhouetted
in the window with her preposterous hats and palm-
leaf fan. At night, the women danced cheek-to-cheek
and men listened to the radio with their arms in slings
or with one empty trouser leg pinned up to their
waist. Singapore fell to the Japanese on 15 February
1942. Siddy remembered this day because her
youngest son was crushed by the milkcart horse. The

horse had knocked him down and trampled him. Siddy came out to the street, her face twisted in disbelief. She carried his small body inside. What she imagined was her soul hurt in a hundred different points of consciousness.

For Paddy, the oldest, the keeper of children, it was worse. She would always have the squalid visions of failure shuddering through her perceptions of herself. No one spoke of her carelessness, but in every respect, she was cautious and despairing. As she grew more beautiful, she grew more morbid, inexhaustibly vigilant for consequence and threat. As if to bring additional weight to the argument, this was not the first child to die. Strong evidence supported the plausible idea that Paddy could not be trusted.

Siddy took the boy's body back to the old town that Joe Flood had taken her to so many years ago. She buried him in the plot next to Nip, his brother. She knew she would come back to this town, it was the nearest thing to home. "My boys are buried next to the bushranger's wife," she told the priest. She sought biblical commentaries, she believed in the distribution of loaves and fishes. God was a charismatic figure to Siddy, but the devout person she was had withered.

After this death, she was electrified by a new idea and she gave herself licence to propagate it. It was Siddy at her most magnetic. She was liquidating her beliefs. It was certainly a historic decision. There was no God. Siddy proved so brilliant, witty, agreeable, keen, affable on the subject of no God that the very vanguard of Sydney low-life gathered to listen. Painters, musicians, philanthropists, writers and individuals whose intelligence was in the nine-minute egg category. They sat on the wobbly chairs that Joe Flood had mended, and drank Mantel's whisky while Siddy served their new cuisine. She hired cooks who could prepare something different, pots of stewed goat with stuffed grape leaves. Until three in the morning the distinguished assembly sang songs. The piano was closed, and spread out on it was an array of liquor in a variety of bottles. Mantel was pissed to the eyeballs and could not drink her large black coffee or eat her dish of prunes.

It was here, at the cafe, that Paddy met Frankie Wilt. She was seventeen and, in her wilful way, she wanted him passionately. He had changed his name from Weinberg. "I use my mother's maiden name," he told her. Against the advice of the aunties, she married him. She, in her violet suit with matching shoes and he, adjusting the RAAF insignia on his uniform for the camera. A week later, he went to war.

Impersonators all around Sydney were calling themselves the Führer. Siddy Church acquired an importance, she provided work during the city's chronic labour shortage, she bought things, mostly buildings, old pubs, pavilions sagging with age, where servicemen came to stand as you eat and give the name and dates of major battles.

Paddy left the cafe and the aunties. She took the

train to Melbourne to live with Frankie's mother, Alice Wilt. She found a place of her own and waited for the war to be over. In October 1944, she gave birth to a daughter, Eadie. Paddy could not have been more pleased. When Frankie came back from the war, he was as sick as a dog and, as Siddy said, "that really buggered up everything."

Paddy said she tried but all she wanted was to go back to her mother. "It's the hormones," said Frankie's mother, "give it a bit longer." Siddy wrote that they would sell the cafe in Sydney and buy the hotel in their old town. She invited them, that is, Paddy and Frankie, to come and live with them but Frankie, still in hospital, wouldn't have a bar of it.

"I'm going home to live with my mother," she told him. His response was immense. Before she could give any details he had a coughing fit that opened his operation and caused him to spit blood. The nurse ushered her out and Paddy rode the bus home with new resolve. Without another word, she took baby Eadie and her suitcase and abandoned married life for a good while. So the marriage stopped before it started, and Eadie Wilt got to be brought up in the pub.

All Eadie would remember was the big old hotel with no daddies and many aunties. The aunties fondled, wrapped and weaned her; guided, misled, prompted and belittled her. They fed, warmed, sheltered and disappointed her and, much more than this, they beguiled and awed her. She in turn would delight and mesmerise, infuriate, fondle, worship, defile, nurse and bury them at last. With them, the earth, the sun and light moved. But she did wonder about daddies.

"They arrange everything. They grabbed our time. They fucked us over. Daddies are all right if they go off to work."

The monologue of daddies had a primitive mystery, and Eadie was not sure that she would like one. Not really understanding murder, rape and sadism or real violence. But these daddies sounded miserable and mucky and she was afraid of the big-penis stories and the walled-up crazy virgins, ripped to shreds by radiant beasts with great tired backs that always needed rubbing and "wipe their bums too," chorused the aunties in the kitchen with dishrags.

From the beginning it was understood, though there is nothing that you can say for certain, it was understood that the child was different. Some said exceptional. And then again, others said backward.

· She knew things. A listening for the energies that disappeared into the cracks of the structure.

Her understanding, said her grandmother, was sneaky fast. The hollow decisions of the adults around her could be put right. She could bring awful days to a sacred ending. Write it down, came to her early around the time she had the rabbit books from the library. There is no substitute for plain story, spoke inner voices piped through her subconcious.

A besotted paradise existed in her snowdome head, thought her mother, Angry Paddy. The mother looked at her drooling child, in ecstasy over an illustration of starry seas, and to her aggrieved eye she looked stupid. Her oohing was the swoon of an idiot and she steadfastly mispronounced words that did not mean anything. She slapped the child and lifted her by the hair from the table to the bed. Torrential anger unravelled in the velvety nights that stretched before them for years and years until the older woman, in an instant, died.

The child took other mothers. Avoiding the ones with creepy-sincere eyes. She chugged off, a slightly battered girl on a mysterious and terrible quest. A dizziness sometimes drowned her. The voices in her head, the incomprehensible chatter haemorrhaged into her days. Muddy words sprang from her lips and howled in her ears, the unique language of other knowing.

The Boulevard of Broken Dreams

Frank Wilt finally folded his pyjamas into the gladstone bag and shaded his smoky eyes from the light of day. He crossed the boulevard feeling poetically dishevelled. The parched blank street at the gates of the Repat Hospital was called The Boulevard by the patients who walked in pairs up and down to test their legs and finger their stitches. They crutched along, reading time backwards, smokes hanging from dry snakey lips. In the ward, Frank was a favourite, mightily young, with ideas of shit and fire, and promise bursting from within his Montgomery Clift face.

He was a beautiful boy, twenty-something. He had hardly any lungs left, a permanent woundedness but his bird-blue genitals shone in the dark. When the other inmates saw his wife and his mother-in-law, they recognised the plethora of disaster that surrounded him. They watched him lying there, cloudy-eyed, listening for the soft sounds of his own breathing. When he did not die, it was reason enough to commemorate him as a contemporary prophet, at least in their ward.

By spring, he knew that his wife and child had gone off. A new nurse was recruited specifically to generate new ideas and inject some life and enthusiasm into the boy in bed sixteen. Responding to forces other than gravity, the ebb and flow of the tides, the universal law: "If you push something," he said, "it pushes back." His recovery was much accelerated by the regular and predictable manner in which the nurse fell in love with him and was the same in all directions, a gravitational force because he needed then to be loved, with some uniformity.

With wanton ritual, she washed the angry red scar that whipped down his body from shoulder to hip. This was where they reached in and hauled out all that good breathing, leaving a blackhole of gasps and sighing. The resident priest from the hospital announced him gone or almost that way.

Frankie did not mind being blessed a Christian, all frames of reference being equally valid, but he intended to distinguish himself by living. He did live! To be exactly twice the age he was on the day he was blessed.

Eadie Wilt, his daughter, just then born, would bury him. She wrote on his slab, twenty-something years later, "Anybody who moves at a constant velocity through space is entitled to regard themselves as stationary." No one knew what it meant and so they pretended it wasn't there, and Eadie did not care because she had a lot of people to bury just around then.

Frankie Wilt was fifty and had lived twenty-five years more than was expected. He had adopted the habit of counselling his own body and had taught himself to breathe in new ways from strange books that travelled in battered boxes to all the rooms he lay down in and called my place.

"Psychological exercises to get in character", he said, helped him to behave like a man intending to live. At the end of his life, at that time when crazy notions are dismissed as theory and the stretching of time makes a mathematical package of a small life. It was said that Frankie would be missed because radiance gives everyone a lift.

If you wished to see from what material he was made, you could return from The Boulevard hospital with him to the home of his mother, Alice Wilt. She had married Frankie Weinberg and gave him an extremely happy life. She had the original startling ice-blue eyes with sooty borders that her son Frankie had inherited so distinctly. In her tiny house down Greville Street you could find new beliefs that could cause you to experience life in a different manner. When Frankie closed the front door and took in the bizarre wild-at-heart smell of his mother's corridor, he felt his senses erupting. Alice Wilt did not hear him come in and was at that moment trying to lift her enormous gurgling mother-in-law out of the bath. It was not going well and they were grunting and heaving in a quirky laconic way. One as large as the other was small – so to speak – two extremes. This went on every day and both were comfortable with it.

In the doorway, little Frankie, now well-educated

in death and the language of the barracks, waited to
be noticed. His old grandma, her filmy body, all vein
and glassy membrane, was being heaved from the
bathtub by a tiny woman who resembled the Duchess
of Windsor, Mrs Simpson.

"Mum?"

The little woman lost her grip and the giant whale
of a woman slid back into the bath. Wedged in, with
an overflow of obscenities that fertilised the room.

Frank did not have any misgivings about taking
his mother's name. His father would have done it too
if it had been the custom. She was the leader of the
family, the drive, the code of logic and certainty from
which they sprang. Her satanically ironic jargon could
not diminish her flair for fidelity. In the narrow world
she inhabited, all let themselves be dazzled by her.

So young Frankie was home, his wife Paddy had
gone back to live with her mother, taking little Eadie
with her.

Alice Wilt's sisters came to visit. To see Frank at
table with the Wilt sisters was visually spectacular. The
Wilt sisters all had wavy chestnut hair, all seven of
them, and sooty-lashed oceanic eyes. They sang in harmony on country radio, and on Sundays they all sat
on a long bench in Alice's kitchen and played banjos,
ukuleles, mandolins, harmonicas and zithers. Alice put
on the roast in the late morning and at two o'clock,
they all ate in the tiny kitchen. Old great-grandma was
spruced up and sat in, with her hair slicked down and
parted with bobby pins, her great backside taking up

far too much bench space. Her husband, The Pa, had died already – Mr Weinberg. He had been a chimney sweep. It was a comfortable living, he monopolised the trade in Melbourne. Only rich people got someone else to sweep their bloody chimneys. He found a leather pouch of gold sovereigns in the Chirnside chimney and the rewards of that had bought this house in St Edmonds road, just off Greville Street, and new long-handled brushes for his sweep that he had made especially at the Blind Institute. Just after this good thing happened, he got run over by a horse-and-cart under the Port Melbourne bridge. When they brought him home, he lay in the parlour all sooted up. He had been on his way home from work. Alice Wilt got the chip heater going and they carried him out to the washhouse and gave him a good scrubbing. Grandpa Weinberg was attended by all the beautiful Wilt sisters with the chestnut hair. They scrubbed him and rubbed their Ponds face cream into his dead face. He lay in the parlour all Sunday and they played gentle songs around him. Sweet harmonic ballads of yearning and lament. He looked as if he'd like to start again.

When Frankie returned to the fold after the war, he was surprised that so little had changed. He stayed absolutely still in the family imagination.

"He knows nothing of really important problems. He is young," spoke the house.

There were food stamps and his sister Nancy drew

black lines up the back of her legs with eyebrow pencil to make them look as if they were sheathed in the coveted silk stockings.

Gangs of children still gathered after dark outside the house because the house was situated adjacent to the streetlight. The fence leaned in where the children sat against it, smoking cigarettes and watching the endless cricket match in progress. From time to time a ball would lob in the front garden and occasionally, through a window.

Frankie Wilt had perfected his fast bowler style out there under the streetlight. He became so good that he was shortlisted for the Test team when war was declared. All his silver cups and newspaper clippings lined the shelves in the front room.

The poster that he had painted for the competition that was held for the opening of the city baths was there. His first prize was framed beside it. If he cared to, he could review himself, his progress, in the front room; the deception of frequently transferred identity, the impaired chronological record of himself. Endless misty-eyed photographs of himself in RAAF uniform, the family at the table on birthdays, the blue-eyed Wilts staring into the camera. They spoke of Hitler and Goebbels but there were other tyrants waiting in the wings.

The penetration of loudness in the centre of a leap had changed Frankie Wilt and no one could much talk to him any more.

"The universe has only a limited number of life

cycles to choose from," he told his mother, "and they all look much the same."

He thought of what happened in the air, in the harbour, on the wharf, at the anti-aircraft batteries, in the camp and the hospital. He knew he was not "fixed up".

One memorable Christmas Day, out in front of Mantel's Cafe, Frankie was in his all-whites. Fast-bowling Frankie, the streetboy with the deadly twist in his ball, was enjoying his last game. His new bride Paddy was watching from the sidelines. Distant relatives were in the camps in Poland. Here, the sun was hot and dry. For Frankie, it was a sensual gypsy feeling, this tension of unrest and threat. No one spoke then of Commander Mitsuo Fuchida or the warships carrying squadrons of bombers preparing to pass from the Celebes through the Banda Sea to the Timor Sea.

Frankie was a sweet lusty boy already in uniform when, on leave in Sydney, he met Paddy. She was riding a bike with her sister Beryl. It was the sister that he wanted. In those hurried times, he was separated quickly from his central fire. It was a question of reflex, the great certainties of life were lost. He slid down the slippery slopes of Paddy's black reasoning, into her perverse moonstance, a raging paradise of furies, a frenzy in the void of a sentence. A profound love ceremony fuelled by her sacred instinct for believing in the very worse outcome of everything.

Her sister's pale Aryan mood, her breathless, complacent sister alliance, her very optimism and

sculptured good looks repelled him. He stroked her hair and went to bed. He dreamt of Paddy's black eyes, her Zapata moustache, her feverish cheeks and heavy brows. In the absence of vigilance, he had come into collision with her look. He knew that she lived with a dread and the decadence of lingering damnation.

Everyone had a good laugh about Paddy's dispossessed *voodootec* but she was too exquisite and inscrutably innocent. She trammelled on the imagination. Never mind that she did not bother to remove facial hair – her sneer was beguiling, her sulk and frown made her a cult heroine, without a cult. The boys that came to the cafe called her, in quiet sniggers, Pandora's Box, but they very soon stopped this around him. He was drowning in her mecurial regrets. You could catch the winds of their unfolding sexuality. You could smell the odour of their damp clothing. Everyone was picking up on it, unfolding in the sanctuary of their appetite, the foreplay of pleasure, the violent foretaste of going down, down into the shadowy hollows and ancient sleepings of submission. The scream, the terror, the land of sacrifice and truly mucky sex. Paddy was seventeen and they divided the path, the unifying light of revolt, they fucked everywhere. On the sands, at the back of the church, in cars, up trees. It was endless, his knees hurt. She put her hand in his coat pocket when they went to the pictures. She had never been seen in a good mood and people thought this might change everything, but her moods stayed black, her conversation could fracture, her demented sombre glance never showed a trace of dancing, joy or bursts of laughter. So there he was in love with one sister and not the other. He moved within her family of women easily. It was very like his own. They had opened their cafe on 23 August 1939, the day Molotov and Ribbentrop signed the Nazi–Soviet non-aggression pact on the backs of Poland and the Western democracies. This was what his future mother-in-law told him as he helped lace Mantel's stays one Sunday morning.

He started up the cricket games on the beach in the salty spray and Frankie did his awesome thing, his devastating fast bowl and people remembered him forever. The circular motion of his arms charged with sweetness and sex. The swimmers dripped and great feelings of potent force lifted them for the afternoon.

He painted the sign for the shop with a row of working women in trousers, hands on hips facing out to sea, arms linked. They were ten times bigger than life size and drew people like flies.

Siddy Church was papering the walls. Little whiffs of calm rapped at the window. Her future son-in-law was tidying her books. He was a wizard with numbers. The wallpaper flew across the walls, a constellation of birds and flowers.

The shop was only closed on Sunday. The war folded around on itself, the world held its breath. The Air Force boy with so few hours in the air came less often on leave.

The war and its characters were in a different universe. A few brave souls staggered back from a distant place.

Every night, Siddy Church would dance a touching cheek-to-cheek with Mantel. Part waltz, part tango, they slithered silently across the polished floor in the early evening before the crowds arrived. People that were drawn together by fate or accident. Between the tables and dancing women sat beautiful bewildered boys, unstable old European men, Austrians and Hungarians who spoke of political murder and terrorism. A table of Jewesses from Berlin and Munich had adopted the sunfrock and other bolder habits of recruitment to the Australian life.

Siddy Church had a code: allow people their prejudices. When people first saw Siddy and Mantel, they saw a pair of hand-holding spinsters but they were a romantic couple.

The war went on for years and years. You could not really know what was going on, said Siddy. At each table there was a different story. The National Socialist table had a copy of *Mein Kampf*. No one knew what that was but the table quoted from it in German and were usually overtaken by the Czechs or the aunties who roared out of the kitchen in great numbers. A watchmaker, called Emile, claimed to have been an early member of Hitler's SA, the brown-shirted razor-gang. "I know," said Siddy, "and I'm the Virgin Mary."

This Emile was repeatedly banned but he kept

coming with his swastika inside his coat, and everyone laughed at him and called him a bludger. The apparitions of war, the endless parade of Goerings, Goebbels, Hitlers, the different groups and shades of opinion lay outside any real authoritative knowledge of the Third Reich. Here, in this remote place, you could still dance till dawn and have leisurely, though heated, discussions with strangers. You could fall in love with anyone you liked. The whole damn mess of the war whirled around in people's brains, the history, the geography, the earthquake of war. Always a sabotage in the air, who to distrust, who to hate. The earth turned.

"Revolution is not a permanent condition," said Siddy. She was cooking a leg of lamb. Paddy made apple-sauce and listened to her mother and the other conversations drifting into the kitchen from the cafe. "Pass the salt," said Siddy.

Sometimes at night crackling radio with insatiable appetite carried speeches and everyone stopped dancing.

Paddy married Frankie Wilt in Melbourne. They all caught the train, all the aunties and Siddy and Mantel. Joe Flood gave her away and looked darkly handsome in the photographs. They rented a small house near Alice Wilt, and Paddy set up housekeeping of her own. In this new city, she was as anonymous as a blade of grass. She went about with Alice Wilt, her mother-in-law, until she started retching and knew she was pregnant. Complete nausea made her forget her longing – her missing the aunties and the mother that she lied to. She shivered at night alone when Frank went back after short leave. A winter flu seemed to sit in her tear ducts; the sky falling down on her head, little noises in the depths of the armchairs. She went from gas stove to the bed to the table, frightened of the thing she carried inside of her.

She gave birth, delirious, her mouth floated around big vowels and consonants. No hyphens. Words full of milk like boats. A tiny magnet cry. A warm descending cry warning her of something. So there I was, little Eadie Wilt covered in the paste of birth, sniffing life. Mother's ankles still swollen, her lips sealed, her ovaries flaying, her nostrils wet. This is the beginning of your world, she whispers, and brings her mouth to the child's heart and looks down at her hollowing belly. Frankie Wilt was a prisoner of war. Alice Wilt had the papers. Paddy had cried over them. She thought she missed him. Too much had happened, for Paddy. She walked around holding her baby and thought of her brother and how she should have been holding him the day he ran out under the milkcart horse. She thought of her brothers and sister on the river in the old house, the pollen-filled mornings. She looked at little Eadie and she knew why her mother cried about her dead babies. With hawk-eye, she sat guarding her newborn. The sun rose. She re-read the last letter that she had received from Frankie Wilt. She told Alice Wilt that everything was dying, staccato style, her brothers and beautiful Frankie. Alice was worried about this slim dark girl. They made milk custard and sweet tea. Dark notions were Paddy's specialty. Alice breathed a cleaner, fresher air. Frankie Wilt arrived back home from the war on 4 October 1945. It was his daughter's first birthday. He lay on his back at The Boulevard hospital and waved at Paddy, who was not allowed into the room but sat at the window, due to his tuberculosis.

For Her Least Look

In the house of my mother Paddy, still an energetic girl then, a combination of robustness and bleak moodiness attracted passers-by cruising for sweet grasses in the flawed gardens of long war years.

For her least look, her fierce emerald quartz glare, we, the other, in her world would shrink small or be glad and nimble. Her look could make colours ripen. Her manners were rude, her eyes flinty, even with shoulders bare and her summer dress irrepressible. It was always like that even before I was there, born alive, with cravings of my own. The air was bright and though men spit blood, *Wonder Woman* comics flooded the newsstands. The war-time economy offered industrial jobs to women, and, for a brief while, Paddy flourished. The working woman was the icon. Beneath orange tile rooftops, Rosie the Riveter, while not belonging to the feminist intelligentsia, hid her pregnancy beneath the pleats of wide trousers.

I imagine that my mother's pregnancy gradually enveloped her in its mists. She worked long hours with machinery and went out dancing with her work companions, the icons, the patriots, butterflies that would return to the chrysalis when the men came home, the larval state.

She was not under the crunch of any man's boot unless it be the great chiding tyrants that swarmed and hauled themselves across the earth. By 1944, the crowing red flares crouched down and turned to a sallow flicker. Hitler had forsaken the lofty spaciousness of the Reich Chancellery. No more rich carpets or mountain views. For a while, the isolation and gloom of a northern forest in a remote province and then, the massive concrete bunker embedded in the ground.

On a distant island – one that Hitler never mentioned – while in a spell, this girl soon to be my mother, slouched her way through strumpet nights. Dancing with simple girls and brides that shriek out, shrill, after a lean day's work, mad to do violence on themselves.

While gold fillings from teeth were melted down and shipped with other valuables, wedding rings of Jews, to the Reichsbank, Eadie Wilt waited to be born.

Benito Mussolini was strung up by partisans. Jewish girls were injected with typhus.

Decades of humour sprang from this era; Hitler's hysterics were already widely cartooned while lives were squandered.

Hitler ate his plate of rice. In the bunker, his Alsatian bitch, Blondi, a gift from Bormann, sprawled at his feet. Like everyone else there, she suffered from intense boredom.

He sat over his maps, between rages, his eyes popping; he would quote Frederick the Great: "Now I know men, I prefer dogs."

Paddy prepared to go to hospital. She packed her grudges, mournful and inconsolable as ever, haughty but not silent, she gave birth in the twilight of the war. Men were returning to their homes, people were no longer armed with "isms". They had lost their footing.

For her least look and her smell of tangerines, my father, Frankie Wilt, would have died in a blue current of recovery. In his torture like a dead man, he cried for her least look, her icebox smile. It astounded his soul that he had a memory of her, in the terrible screaming winds of war. He was not in good shape, brown as a leaf; he now weighed five stone, the weight of a child.

Frankie Wilt was a chocolate soldier. His war was twenty-year-old boys, Betty bombers, and red-hot metal falling around him. Box brownie reproductions of wasted boys in the tropics in bamboo cages. On the world stage, Frankie Wilt's war was a backwater. Everyone spoke of Hitler, no one knew of Mitsuo Fuchida. Frankie's war was black smoke, shattered harbours. Blossoming anti-aircraft bursts below him. Flying pieces of metal and the acrid smell of burning flesh. The earth shuddered. Deplorable chaos. Time passed meltingly slow. Arms severed from torsos in slow motion. The Timor Sea, Bathurst Island, twenty-seven aircraft in triangular formation at eighteen thousand feet. From the trenches, they trespassed stupidly and then the dysentery, the gangrene. The brooding pidgin English of the captors. The laconic smiling "Number One" speak of the Japanese commanders. The taste of mucus and blood. Young boys galloping into old age on this little turf somewhere near Java. The perfumed jungle simmering.

A long time after, when everyone had died and Eadie Wilt looked through the boxes of photographs and keepsakes of her family, she found bits of story. The neat stack of love letters with the wartime cartoon graffiti crossing the envelopes.

During brief visits years later with her vagabond father, she asked him about the war. He was light on detail. The conversations were flat and full of dark advice.

"Our plane crashed near a black lake," he cross-hatched. There was a dignity to his hedging.

"There were twelve of us alive. We sat on this island and waited for the Japs to get us. We burned all documents likely to give useful information to the enemy and hid our weapons. We didn't know where we were . . . somewhere near Java. We were going to make a stand against the Japanese. Starvation was gobbling up our strength. There was a five-seater plane a few miles away on the other side of the island. It had been abandoned but we had the wild idea that we could get it going, it gripped us."

He smiled shyly and looked up at her.

"Yes, it gripped us. Of us twelve, two were blind with shattered faces, another had his hands amputated and the other was paralysed from the waist down. Anyway, the plane responded and we prepared to fly."

"Did you all fit in?"

"No, only five."

"Who did you leave behind?"

"We drew names out of a hat, the rest stayed."

"And your name was one of the five?"

"Yes, myself, the two blinded, the handless and the paralysed boy . . . we five. Seven healthy boys stayed to meet the Japanese and we never saw them again." But . . . Eadie wanted to protest what was already put to rest.

"Those were the names that came out of the hat, Eadie," he cautioned.

Eadie already knew that all had later died except Frankie and his friend, Mr Honeywell, who had no hands. He painted watercolours with the brush between his teeth and smoked cigarettes from a bamboo splint that had been devised in Nakom Patom in 1942. He always said he was lucky because he couldn't dig latrine pits in the camp. When Frankie was recuperating from something on the lung, the wives of the seven boys came to see him, and he told them about the names in the hat.

Seven mothers came to see Frankie. They looked at his blistered feet and though they couldn't enter the room, they sat at the little window and asked about his septic sores and scrotum trouble. They asked how he had lost so many teeth. Japanese soldiers in the camp went in for an orgy of face slapping. They had left him with an endearing smile, a broken keyboard smile. "I think it was the rice polishings and the soybeans," he answered. The seven mothers brought vivid flowers and took pleasure in Frankie being alive. He had dreams of slow running streams with grassy edges. In his dreams, he ate snakes and centipedes, scorpions and huge tarantulas. In his dreams, he had artificial legs constructed out of bamboo. In his dreams, he had every disease, dysentery, malaria and cholera. Every type of fly settled on him, in his dreams, his mouth was blown and maggoty. Troops of monkeys swung past flowering trees of brilliant colour, the vague perfumes of freesia, locusts and butterflies flecked with light filtered through his dreams.

There were drawings that Frankie had sent on envelopes to Paddy during the war, drawings of flare-ups of brutality with a clandestine humour that seemed like a confidence trick. Tiny men, bayoneted through their chests, drawn in detail. Eadie puzzled over their cruelty, twenty years after her father had died. Frankie came back with his head of wires. He stood in the big hush of Paddy's will-she-won't-she landscapes and waited for her to restore his radiance. For eighteen months, he sat in his downy blue pyjamas and drew pictures with Derwent pencils. They fed him and washed him well. His wife and child went off and he didn't see them for six years.

During that time for one reason or another Paddy changed her ways. Sometimes she forgot to be perfect. Sometimes she cried in her beer and told everyone that Frankie Wilt was the only man she ever loved. Everyone nodded their heads and agreed that she'd lost a good sort. This reponse was enough to make her reverse the lament and list his shortcomings to anyone who would listen. Sometimes she became so angry that she gritted her teeth and dragged Eadie from her bed by her hair.

Eadie liked to think about all the handless people that painted with the brush held between their teeth.

"There must be thousands of them," she told Grandma Siddy. Making them common as swans, unexceptional and plentiful, made her feel better about herself and her idle hands.

Life at the big old hotel went on with Siddy, Joe Flood, the aunties and Mantel. Paddy worked long hours; her long red nails were chipped and her beautiful sorrowful face shadowed and stained. Eaten away by a viciousness, knocked out of her right mind. Everyone waited for the miraculous repair. Siddy told Eadie that Paddy had been a dazzlingly earnest child who took care of her brothers and sister. Stories passed from woman to girl, worming themselves into niches.

Paddy told Eadie on a blind winter night that when Siddy came home and found Nip dead, she had taken

Paddy's hand and ripped out a fingernail. Such witchery scared the piss out of Eadie.

When her mother grew distraught she lay in her small bed on the other side of the room and listened to the anger, the black intractable hiss of anxiety and fear.

During That Time

Paddy came back to her mother's house which was really a hotel, and the aunties said that she was mad. She carried a pretty baby that infuriated her with its unflinching gaze.

No one bothered to explore the origins of Paddy's so-called madness. It became a slightly sordid and irritating factor in the daily life at the pub. At first, everyone was pleased when Paddy had a few drinks. The monumental intensity softened and she would laugh and sing, paint her face with boot polish and stand on the piano in her father's suit and sing all the old classics. Everyone loved her then, that beautiful toothsome smile, abandoning her domineering fury to the absent-mindedness of drink.

As the years went by, Eadie grew from a pretty baby into a wiry child. Paddy stayed as furious as ever. The aunties had developed a strategy to protect the child from the mother's outpourings of rage. Everyone preferred the child to roam free in the wooded hills behind the hotel, to climb trees, anything out of earshot of her mother. When Paddy moved toward her daughter, the aunties were alert, swooping down, great top-heavy birds, all wings flapping, feathers that Paddy got stuck in and was moved along by.

No one blamed Paddy, everyone knew the shades of melancholy; the women recognised a disappointed soul. Her ugly moods were fragile, her struggle dictated her behaviour. She said she lived bitter hours. She said she did not know why she was angry. She began quite early to look for a disease, and her search became ruthless after she turned forty. By that time, her daughter Eadie had a child of her own.

The aunties were dead or very old; Eadie still remembered what Siddy told her, against the garden wall where they bared their knees and closed their eyes to the sun. "The God-holy truth," said her grandmother Siddy, "is that you are going to have one great and marvelous life."

Their eyes were close, noses touching.

"Do you believe me?"

Eadie believed her grandmother in a big way. The old hand took the filthy child's fingers into her palm and gave no reasons.

Paddy did remember being happy, she talked about it. "During that time," she said, "I did not feel angry." She incessantly said, "during that time," in her circular mirror, she told herself, "then I was quite happy." She referred to the times, perhaps, of her early marriage, when she leapt out of the family pocket. She decided that "during that time" was worthy of remembrance.

It was not just the man, though he was grandly

young and blazing enough. It had more to do with Alice Wilt. When Alice first met her daughter-in-law, she murmured, so all could hear, "lovely lovely".

Alice saw the melancholy but she did not object to that. She had worked all her adult life in the knitting mills with hundreds of migrant women. Women with bitter slanting mouths who came from countries where camels passed and men beat their wives every day. She did not distrust young girls with wounded hearts, they were in a good place with her, they sang in unison. Paddy and Alice took size eight in dresses and size five-and-a-half in shoes. They both had trim ankles and walked rapidly, almost a run, at all times. When the son introduced the bride to his mother, she said aloud "lovely" and Paddy coloured dark pink along her throat and her cheeks throbbed with heat. The women went about together. Paddy would make curried egg sandwiches and meet her mother-in-law outside the factory. They would sit on the strip of green next to the railway line and eat, then they would walk down Chapel Street past the Astor Theatre and look for bargains. The narrow hips swayed valiantly and people said, "They are of the same mould." Paddy thought every day of her mother and said she missed her, she ironed her petticoats and ate her breakfast all alone. Every day she woke up and said, "I am awake today," and smoked a cigarette.

Frankie was away and Alice lived nearby. Paddy's pregnancy and the war increased her feeling of being buried alive. Yet she still said, "During that time I was happy." She came home oily from the machines. She was something of a whiz with machines, they said. She sat next to Alice on the tram that rattled down High Street and read the headlines, and they argued freely on the most interesting and instructive subjects.

She continued to be morbid, to have a distaste for just about everything, but that did not bother Alice Wilt: she went about her business of liking everything and the two women got along very well.

Alice was very disappointed later, when the marriage did not work out; she had wanted to see Paddy for her whole life.

"It wasn't to be," she told her grand-daughter.

Eadie Wilt was highly impressed that her Grandma Alice thought so much of her mother.

They made clothes for each other and gossiped languidly over the sink. They prepared tea for old Great-grandma and The Pa, who was still alive and kicking then. After tea, they would sit on the verandah and smoke Alice's Turf cigarettes and watch the kids playing cricket under the streetlight. They would walk in their aprons and slippers and buy something sweet at the milk bar for Alice's husband, Big Frankie, who was getting bigger everyday from his craving for sweets. Alice indulged him, she liked to spoil him and no one talked about health then.

The women walked slowly home, stopping at number seven and number thirty-three to talk to the Jewish woman who was an expert on the war and the woodman who had just come back from the

Dandenongs with some mallee roots. Their apron pockets were full of Mars Bars and Violet Crumbles, and they smoked all the way, sometimes linking arms, casting their shadows across the gardens as the sun went down. This was the legendary happiness that Paddy had been permanently marked by.

Paddy may have seen then, what it might mean to be sure of who you were.

The ravaging gravity in Paddy's face, where did it come from? As she grew older, Eadie saw her mother's legacy creeping into her own life, but back then, she grew as contradictory as possible; it was her only defence.

During this time, when Paddy strolled nightly with Alice, Eadie wasn't even born yet. Paddy enjoyed the days when nothing happened. She had passionate encounters and cut her long hair. She and Alice Wilt kept the promises they made to each other. Alice reconciled her household to the disruptive influences of a tormented and passionate woman. Their fidelity to each other was final and lasted a lifetime, even though they only passed messages to each other through Eadie at the last. They knew of each other's griefs and defended each other in the skirmishes and turmoil that inscribe a family history.

When Eadie Wilt was born, she jumped straight into the arms of Grandma Alice. If she could have seen through the membrane that still filmed her vision, she would have seen the sweet boney smile of the woman she would love the best. Grandma Alice had a way of going to the head of the line in the love stakes. Everyone loved her the best.

She would eventually have many grandchildren, but this was her first and she was privileged. She wore the name that Alice chose for her, and would later be shown where truth lies if you have the strength to grasp it.

It was October. The children played cricket in their bathers and she put on the sprinkler and wet them all. The men were still away and the new child had the blue eyes of a china doll.

When Eadie had grown a bit, the women from Alice's factory took her on a picnic. They wore their trousers and work boots and got mucky collecting mushrooms. Eadie Wilt had just started to smile and blow raspberries. The women passed her around and packed the mushrooms that they had collected all around her. They swam in the muddy river and ate boiled eggs with salty fingers. Alice Wilt and Paddy talked of serious and sensual things.

Alice said later, "Women can talk filthy . . . like men have never heard!" And she cackled and stooped to pick up a pin on the street. Alice Wilt always picked up pins on the street, her shopping cart was full of pins. "It is good luck," she told her grand-daughter, "though this is something you won't need, my darling Eadie."

Alice Wilt spent a great deal of time with the chip heater. She was always foraging for small pieces of wood to start it. In her basket were leaves and chips. Other larger branches stuck out at all angles. Dragging bits of tree trunks down the street really irritated Paddy, and she refused to get her violet gloves soiled. The matters of drains and plumbing greatly interested Alice Wilt. She climbed on the roof to clean the drains and found out what was what. The rainwater was not getting to the tanks. She could spend the whole weekend on the roof, she liked it up there; it was another country. It was the same with wood, she wanted four sizes, she said. Firstly, small twigs. Then, bigger branches. Split logs, and finally nice solid lumps of red to burn long and hot. The concern and collection of wood had an episodic nature because she had to constantly come back to it.

Alice was always looking for building sites that had timber off-cuts lying around. This obsession had a practical value; it was to ensure that the chip heater worked perfectly to give people instant hot baths. Alice's bathroom was outside in the laundry. There were no electric lights. Candles and an oil lamp, the spluttering crackling and smoking of the old iron-mother made it a delightful experience the first time around. The steam from the water rose and frosted the windows as the bather undressed awkwardly and stood shivering on the bare cold floor. The wind whistled through the planks and sometimes Big Frankie passed by the window with his bushy black eyebrows.

On Sunday afternoons, after the roast and the musical interlude, Paddy joined Alice in her bath ritual.

Afterwards, they washed their undies and nylons and played cards. Alice sang in her Vera Lynn voice and Paddy joined in.

The radio turned over the war between melodies that they knew by heart. They ironed the pillow cases and set their hair in butterfly pins for work on Monday. Finally they wrote letters to young Frankie Wilt. They did not know it but he was tied by the ankles in a bamboo cage, scared out of his wits.

Sometime after the baby was born, Siddy Church came to visit. Joe Flood and Mantel and a half-dozen aunties came in the Packard. The child was christened in a lace dress and everyone was glad that her eyes were blue. Photographs were hand-coloured which re-affirmed and stood as testimony forever that the eyes were blue. Everyone had this picture on their piano.

By the time the father had returned from war, the eyes had clouded and were then like moist olives. The grandmothers were united by their devotion and still found the child immensely attractive, blue eyes or no eyes, said Paddy who always had a blunt way of putting things.

They stayed at Alice Wilt's house. Siddy and Mantel and Joe Flood shared the bungalow, which Paddy found profoundly irritating. This bungalow had quite a history and was yet to house a strange collection of peoples down the track, long after this emphatic trio had moved on.

The bungalow had been built for Alice Wilt's mother-in-law, whom people down Greville Street would later refer to as "The Old Jew". In her youth she was vivacious and engaging. Glistening dark eyes and a most unfrivolous nose, large and grandly curved.

"It was an Empress's nose," said Alice. There was a picture of her on the piano in tulle with a lily-of-the-valley in her hair.

Old Great-grandma Chinzy Weinberg liked to live with Alice Wilt, her daughter-in-law especially, after her husband, Pa Weinberg, bought this house and they had some comfort. When he was an apprentice chimney sweep he could slither down the stacks with a brush. He was so small that he hoped to be a jockey. He met his wife at the stables in Punt Road. He took the horses out on Sundays very early along the beach, cantering in the surf. Chinzy's father owned the stables and the horses. He was not keen to have his daughter marry a chimney sweep. She did, however, and had a good life being poor. Just as she grew tired of the poorness, Pa had some luck, and comfort came just in time. Chinzy Weinberg, however, felt destitute when Pa died. She stopped everything except eating and said, "I want to be alone."

No one was startled by this. Greta Garbo had already said it and it could be expected from European women with thick accents and smoky eyes.

Alice Wilt, looking for a solution, had a bungalow built in the back garden and moved Chinzy in there. She did not say she wanted to be alone any more but broke all the rules concerning neighbourly etiquette. Harmless things, like standing in the garden with her big-boned nakedness for all to see. She liked the sun on her great sloping belly and would scratch at her pubic hair and lie in the sun. It was a shame to take her inside, said Alice, she liked it so much, but everyone rang up and talked about it.

"Call the doctor, they are always right and they know better than we do," said the Wilt sisters, but Alice had her doubts about that.

Instead of calling the doctor or bringing Chinzy inside she erected a trellis and grew creeper up the outside and transplanted little trees that she made Big Frankie drive especially to Dandenong for. Chinzy could sit in the sun all she liked and no one could see in. People stopped talking and everything was bliss, until local boys broke through the trellis and stole her jar of threepences. This wasn't so bad, but they called her "The Old Jew" as they ran off, and she refused to sleep in the bungalow ever again.

She wanted to sleep in the armchair in Alice's bedroom, which was much too small for such a large woman. Ever obliging, Alice moved the bed from the sleepout into the house, and to the end of her days Chinzy slept at the foot of Alice's bed. Sometimes waking in the night for a cuddle, like a big old baby, said Alice, as she stroked the elder woman's cheek.

When Alice heard that Siddy was coming to stay, she had to find extra beds quick. She went to the Brotherhood and found some half-decent bases but the mattresses were too stained. She ordered three new, single innersprings and had them delivered from Maple's in Chapel Street. Then she arranged them along each wall of the sleepout.

"You sure have a strange family," said Max from number seven, "three in every bedroom."

"That's true," said Alice.

"Three in every bedroom is too much."

She took Chinzy shopping and the large-breasted peasanty woman held tightly to the lithe aristocratic lady with the sooty-lashed eyes.

"My mother-in-law would like a white-satin bed jacket," Alice told the saleswoman.

She always bought her impractical things. It made up for the mess she got herself in. Alice felt that it balanced things out.

The creative horseplay that went on between Chinzy and Alice annoyed Paddy. Even she knew she was envious.

"Envy springs from belief in lack," said Alice and she dabbed tomato sauce on Paddy's nose and tried to involve her in the food fight that was going on just then. Paddy walked out and slammed the front gate. Alice watched the confrontational strut disappear down the street.

It was difficult for Alice to go to work every day even though Max from number seven kept her eye on things. "She taught me lots of things," she told Paddy about Chinzy who was being especially perplexing that month.

"Like what?" asked Paddy as they boarded the tram, running late again.

"Like Polish dumplings and chicken liver omelettes and how to cure worms with angelica and brandy and Schadenfreude," said Alice barely making it around the word.

"What's that?" asked Paddy.

"That," said Alice, "is the incautious action of having joy in your neighbour's misfortune." Paddy didn't answer. The conductor came with his leather bag and coupons. "Yes," said Alice, "you've got to watch out for that."

The Sleepout

Only those people with reasonably intact memories could list all the incidents concerning Alice's sleepout. Certainly it was built for Chinzy and she liked it well enough. As for the next inhabitant, who it was, no one could say for sure. The veils had fallen and only certain memories would push themselves forward. It was agreed that during the visit of Siddy some curiosities occurred that everyone remembered.

It was stock in trade for Alice to recall this time as the time of many pregnancies. There was Paddy, of course, a vivacious slip of a girl adroitly savouring her foreign bed, a delicate thing with her ripples of fugitive unrest. Two Wilt sisters abundantly chestnut-haired, eating pastries, ant-hills of saccharine endearments and big as buses. One would have twins and the other, a saintly-looking giantess born with long greasy hair whose birth left her mother drained for the rest of the summer.

Last, but not cocooned in leastness, was Max, the friend from number seven, who was named Isola, though everyone called her Max. No one could remember why Isola was called Max. It did not suit her at all and was not an abbreviation of her name.

Therein lies the answer, reasoned Alice. Max was not conspicuously or excruciatingly pregnant. She wore her usual translucent gaze and could still be caught loafing at the knitting mill. As Alice was overseer, Max was never hurried along, and as Alice was always being sacked anyway, the organisms of employment were not disturbed by Max's resistance to any sort of hurried labour and Alice's refusal to extract this hurry from her.

In her youth, she had an astonishing succession of love affairs. This was a woman of tranquil passions. Her virtuoso, fire-eating independence provided all the ingredients for abracadabra happiness.

Sultry-voiced, huskily urgent, stirred and fully aroused, the eye she cast on you swept you away. The lines of convergence that linked Alice Wilt and Max were crucial to the sequences that would augment the families for several decades. For those who did not like Max, the war was a Godsend. With her homeland stolen, the falsification of anecdotes, and the facts of her beauty, a flare-up of prejudice attached itself to her. She folded her arms in challenge. In the meantime, she met and married a ginger-bearded elephantine man called Mr Grollo who announced the epoch of discrimination over. Max was enraptured. Mr Grollo's prospectus, announced in operatic tenor, filled the knitting factory with a gathering momentum. When he was home on leave, they married and honeymooned in an afternoon. The main aim was relaxation in glorious circumstances, he told his transformed bride beneath the ceiling fans of the Renaissance Hotel.

"We did some sightseeing and ate in the banquet facilities," she told Alice.

After he had gone back to service, she felt a certain instability, which was finally diagnosed as pregnancy. Max adapted to the world of Mr Grollo. As it turned out, he was sent home very soon. The street slandered her and her talkative husband; he could corner and explore the unexplored surface of any subject for a long tiresome hour. He was a buff, that is, a ski buff, a music buff, an anything buff.

"Viruses evolve more than a million times faster than cellular organisms, so they don't mutate out of existence," he lectured the doctor on a housecall. Max began to turn out cuisine. There were shrines all around the house and on certain days candles burned all day in the kitchen. Mr Grollo wore his yarmulke and Max kept on at the knitting factory but stopped wearing sunfrocks.

Max no longer walked along St Kilda beach on Saturdays to skate at St Moritz. Good times were extinct. She never loitered at work, and all her sex was in the cooking.

Beautiful, lost Max. If she departed from the strictest orthodoxy or did not fill the cupboard with good things or did not soldier on in spite of the astonishing mediocrity of her intellect (for this is what he told her after the love had become a relic surprised by time) – if she did not, what then?

Alice Wilt, who had a strong sense of social oblig-
ation, visited them every evening after tea to see if his
war wounds were healing. Tchaikovsky beamed
through their front room and out of the wire door
into the street. He liked to talk about Tchaikovsky's
homosexuality and Beethoven's deafness and
Mahler's Jewishness. Max wore a frilly apron and
chopped liver in the kitchen. Alice put her arm
around Max's shoulder and tried to gossip over the
andante cantabile of the string quartet.

She knew that some hostile propaganda had
sprung up in the street, the woodman no longer deliv-
ered wood. The apparatus of ignorance was growing
as quick as Isola's belly, said Mr Grollo, who insisted
on speaking German in the milk bar and told everyone Isola is Isola not Max, though no one could get
used to it at all.

Alice knew something was wrong when Max finished her buttonholes before all the other women,
never took a smoke-break and stopped going to the
Women's Hospital for her checkup.

She just cooked, and what cooking! Mr Grollo was
now out of his wheelchair and devoted his entire
attention to the tasting and perfecting of Isola's cooking. Alice watched her kneading, her belly lightly
dusted with flour.

"Shhhh! 'Pathétique', the last symphony, is playing," instructed Mr Grollo.

Max kneaded dramatically during the first movement but by the fourth she was beyond the brink

of despair and went into labour.

It was a long night. The knöffels came out of the oven, the poppyseeds tasted like heaven. Alice and Max walked. Discarding the man, they convinced him that it was a false alarm. He fell asleep in the armchair and they slipped out of the house.

With some stoicism, Max told Alice that she was not going to hospital to have her baby. In the fairyland of intimate relationships, Alice Wilt and Max did not question the overall picture.

They walked slowly along the street, their arms linked; a threadbare cricket game was still in progress under the streetlights outside Alice's house. Young girls sucking on cigarette butts turned exquisite profiles to the approaching women. They made room for them to squeeze through the gate. Inside, the Wilt pantomime was in mid-performance; paradigms of working-class kitsch. Alice Wilt's grand-daughter would one day write of this household, trying hard for her first form exam essay.

On this night, Eadie Wilt was there, a diminutive dynamo in the heartland of the house, only a few months old. Everyone volunteered to hold the blue-eyed baby. The impressive grandfather held the tot. He swapped her for a Mars Bar that Alice offered him from her apron pocket. Public approval ratings, unburdened by complex child-rearing policies, were a ticking time bomb of adoration.

"This is a spoiled baby," said Paddy who was uncharacteristically soft and teary this night. This was because in the sleepout, transformed by the folksy homilies of Alice Wilt, sat Paddy's mother, Siddy Church. She arrived in caravan style with VIP parody and an auntie chauffeur. Siddy Church and her whole caboodle had arrived for a visit. The sleepout had become the focus of activity. Joe Flood, still handsome but off with the birds, dressed in starched white shirt with gold cufflinks, was propped in the Chrysler with the commodities of travel. He scored points for dapperness but he had to be kept away from Paddy at all times. Everyone knew this instinctively. When they all arrived with much tooting and hauling of luggage, Joe was taken from the Chrysler and installed on his couch-bed in the sleepout with his mandolin. He strummed quietly in the background. Paddy ignored him.

The story that needs to be told – brief though it is since the facts were never accurately known – was this: At some time during Paddy's childhood, when Joe Flood had already well and truly lost his marbles, he had done something to Paddy. Exactly what this something was had never been told. It was, however, serious enough for Siddy to attempt some bodily harm to the man. The repercussions were that Paddy, who had loved her handsome old man, was kept right away from him. No matter how she tried, she could not remember much. Imaginations being stronger that just about anything, the guesswork on the matter was so vibrant that it well exceeded that which actually took place.

It was in the early days when Paddy was an earnest, loving child. She was brushing away flies from her dad's face while he finger-picked his mandolin; miraculous melodies bending and zig-zagging the innuendos of the afternoon. Optimism was what she felt, if she had only known the word, and an Old Testament reverence for her clever, beautiful father. She liked the way he winked at her when his fingers had been especially quick. She knew he was not as clever as he had once been. The confectioneries of his music suggested that the clever ones did not have a currency as knee-jerking as this one.

Quick was what he was being today; Paddy was totally in touch and gave her patronage wholeheartedly. He played and wouldn't stop, and she stayed absorbed and persuaded by his lampooning, finger-licking trills. Love saturated hero worship. Suddenly he stopped dead.

"Quick," he told her, suddenly looking like the stereotype hopeless victim. She realised that he wanted to go to the lavatory which was a fair trip down an L-shaped corridor. She grabbed an old bottle that Siddy used to water the geraniums.

She helped him steady himself at the tiny opening of the bottle, and although some spilt, he closed his eyes and sighed with relief as the bottle caught the acrid stream.

Paddy understood perfectly his "whew". Siddy's annoyance at pissing oneself was enough to upset the house for the week. In fact, she wanted to go badly herself. She looked at him while he was trying to shake it and get it all back in his pants with some degree of order.

"I gotta do it too, Dad," she whimpered.

They both looked down the length of the verandah shiftily. He held the bottle shakily with his two hands bending over trying to keep it steady, his buttons still undone, his shirt-tail all skew-whiff. She squatted over it; her little shivery legs quivered as she tried to pee neatly.

To deny the role of irony and fantasy or plain bad luck would be useless. Siddy came around the bend of the verandah with no desire or expectations to diagnose images, to fix their meaning. What she thought she saw was this airheaded bastard trying to penetrate her daughter with a beer bottle.

Where this interpretation came from no one could guess.

"It was what she saw."

"She saw it with her own eyes."

So that was that. Paddy grew and was kept increasingly busy with the incinerating role of eldest daughter. The penalties of this role may already be guessed at. Paddy could well have had a better time as the youngest child.

When her dad got better from his beating, he went back to playing his tunes but he was not so quick. No one listened to him much. Eadie Wilt took a liking to him round the age of three, when she rocked from side to side and split her sides laughing at his antics.

The old bastard was harmless by now, said the house, and Eadie trusted him completely.

When Alice Wilt met her daughter-in-law's family for the first time, she noticed Paddy's passing over of her father, Joe Flood. She suspected that therein lies the solution. As she was so fond of reasoning in this manner, she became quite occupied with Joe Flood during this visit and Paddy's aversion to him.

It was a night of unusual calm. Alice and Max left Mr Grollo sleeping soundly. They found themselves in the sleepout playing cards with Siddy Church, Mantel Bonlevi and the assorted aunties. Joe Flood had long curled up and Paddy had taken her baby Eadie into the house to sleep.

The moon was predictably bright. The garden bordering the sleepout looked bedraggled from all the comings and goings. At first the women played cards in a vaguely celibate manner, even the aunties with greedy hearts.

The game progressed. Mantel Bonlevi spread her brown spatula fingers across her fan of cards. She had something there, an ace or a flush. She held her evil-smelling cigarette between her teeth. The aunties began hurling bets at her. She collected, sweeping the coins into her corner and licking the point of her pencil to write the score. The others retaliated by banning smoking, collectively, in the sleepout. Mantel went outside for a cough. The mechanical game became subtle and elusive. Each face all of a sudden was interested, one theatrically sceptical, another curious and sly and so on. Apart from that, the talk became wilder: seemingly lunatic notions developed as player after player ambushed the topic and embellished the sublime or ridiculous.

Supper was introduced, everyone sipping tea between deals. There were the scatterings of marzipan, chocolates, caramels and peppermints that often come with aunties, even, it seemed, this tough-cookie, leather-booted variety of auntie. Sipping and groaning with anticipation, the commentaries continued. Granules of understanding caused a raised eyebrow every now and then. Impertinence and praise shifted back and forth across the table.

The women in the sleepout way down on earth, a tiny dot of amber light surrounded by Alice Wilt's velour lawn. Stars and comets; moons and worlds glided past in boundless space. The gathering resembled nothing more than the Mad Hatter's tea party; Ace of Hearts and Two of Hearts, Mantel immodestly winning. All spines were erect, assailed on all sides by questioning human beings holding hors-d'œuvres and pulling sphinx faces. Cards were played in the jungle where Frankie Wilt had given up the fight to be a man. A charred pack was found in the bunker near the body of Hitler's dog, Blondi.

Alice Wilt studied the phenomenon purposefully. By slow degrees omens showed up the frailty of the game. They talked about "mortally ill", "contracted cancer", and the war. The cards kept turning. They

talked about the unrealisable, the magnetising forces
of time passing. Ambition and children and temple
dancing and remarkable decisions that people made.
They talked about all these things. They talked about
frozen meat and "The Greek" and everyone's parent-
age. Knotty problems, ideas and techniques that
worked and experiments that failed. Siddy sang and
fetched the travel flask of whisky. They talked about
having plenty and how things changed but didn't
much at all.

They guessed at hands and trebled their bets. They
could not yet see the whole plot, but they continued to
unlock riddles and beat about the bush. Like dogs
sucking marrow from the bone, thought Paddy, who
had been awakened for the 2 a.m. feeding by Eadie,
her hungry, still blue-eyed baby. When she saw the
light burning in the back yard she came out to see
what the hell was going on. What was going on was all
and everything; the sisterhood was artfully scorching
the laminate top of the sleepout's table. Piles of money
went from side to side. Notions of sacred nonsense
were being feverishly exchanged, camouflaged and
guarded against. From hand to hand passed the lustre
of small hopes. Years evaporated. Allegiances were rig-
orous, the manipulations terrifying. The naked light
bulb hung by its roots. Hands mottled with age shuf-
fled the deck. No one was permitted to sleep.

Directed from far off, it was this dubious night
which ponderously remained in everyone's memory.
The shiftings of the years established that everyone

present took this night very seriously, and, indeed, why not?

This was the night that Max brought a very good card game bodily to a halt with the fireworks of child-birth. It was achieved quickly with the rough-hewn virtues of folk-art. The chip heater blazed and boiled. Everyone breathed and pushed and knew the reasons for universal equilibrium. These reasons were fres-coed across the sleepout's ceiling forever. There was no need that night to debate the existence of the soul. Later everyone was pleased to have personally deliv-ered a baby. Many years later, after hearing repeated scenarios of the phenomenal, stupendous, incompara-ble and improbable miracle, Eadie Wilt felt jealous that she was not the infant born that night.

The girl born was called Nilli, she was to suffer the same cultural quarantine in the street as her parents. They decided to raise her as a good Jewish girl, and the parents travelled by train to synagogue and ate or didn't eat all the proper foods on the proper days. Max was sometimes treated scathingly by the woman in the milk bar. This woman thought that Max was a German and therefore a Nazi. "Jewish" was just starting to sink in, what it was, in Australia. Then, Mr Grollo had a heart attack and died. Max never bothered to be Isola again. She kept up the cooking. She felt she had the gift. As for being Jewish, that, she gradually let slide.

"It was too much trouble," she said. "All right for the men but where's it ever got me?"

Alice Wilt agreed. She never wanted to be anything either. Prayer was something. It helped and angels were nice. She had a picture of one, over her bed, in sepia with a bow and arrow.

Nilli was a dark child with black hair that grew right down the edges of her face and even though angels beat their gossamer wings, she did not have blue eyes. All her life she wanted blue eyes, even though Eadie Wilt had lost hers. She was not old enough to experience the three-minute agony of her father before he was carried out of the house in his ancient tweed jacket. He had not been a lucky man. The fat ambulance shot down Chapel Street and crashed before it reached the hospital. At the funeral service, baby Nilli wailed and Max sang half a lullaby to shush her.

After Siddy Church and her entourage had packed up and gone home, a peace settled on the empty sleepout. It had experienced a wild time, and nothing caused a stir in Alice's back yard until young Frankie Wilt at last came home from the war.

The first time Paddy saw her young husband Frankie home was at the Repat Hospital. She would not believe it was him. She felt so strong, full and able-bodied, and lusty. He was like an eight-year-old boy, all bones and blisters. She pushed through their curfews and quarantines and hugged him decently as he deserved. His body was not obedient, he had the tremors, the shits; a kind of walking shadow that couldn't walk, and he belonged to the nurse. Paddy was only allowed to touch him that once and it broke her heart.

"He has TB," the gorgeous nurse told her. "Your daughter can catch it."

She could sit and watch him from a safe distance. She watched the Amazon-nurse lift him from the bed like a baby, squashed against her Big Bertha breasts. He coughed colourlessly. She watched his face plump out a bit after a time behind the medicine bottles and catch phlegm in his handkerchief, greenish-yellow. She lost her job; the men were coming back, women were leaving the workforce in droves, they were girls again. They bought negligees and put away the sensible shoes.

Siddy Church wrote that they had purchased the big old hotel in the old town, and Paddy reproached herself for exaggerating the importance of big nurse to her little Frankie.

He stopped looking haunted, and in her deepest layers she said, I'm cheated, he's mine. Her childlike vision, her religious credo to take care was strangled by hospital procedure. He was still as light as thistle-down, the weight of her feelings was heavier. Her mouth was down at the edges; he saw her from a distance. To her he could not turn, but he loved her neat black head against the pale green hospital wall. His laughter promised to hold her again. No ordinary human contact, the severance.

"It's bloody stupid," said Alice.

Still, they talked at a distance and made promises that were never kept.

One day she arrived when the nurse was giving him a rub-down. He had come to prize consistency, clinical precision dished out every day by the nurse, who always smelled of soap, who came running when he had nightmares and cried out and shat himself uncontrollably. Siddy Church came to visit with her daughter, saw that he was becoming whole again. She shrewdly suggested a trip home for Paddy. Frankie Wilt was dead against it and raised himself off the pillow. Enough to spit blood and go very red.

"What was happening to them?"

There were days when Paddy hesitated. Then came the inscrutable, exquisitely timed episode that got Paddy thinking about her dubious marriage.

The big nurse was orbiting around Frankie, giving him the confidential purpose of a man in full possession of his powers. His ward had a special atmosphere. The sensuous remounting of young manhood, that's how she saw it.

She was "getting him back in the saddle", she joked.

"One man can do nothing," he spoke particularly quietly and with gravity. He could not talk to his wife like this, he was isolated from her. So the chickens came home to roost, or rather, one day Paddy came but never came again.

Paddy would always remember the morning. She was early, she arrived during his rub-down, she could see his naked body under the oiled hands of the nurse, behind the curtain. She didn't know that he was still struggling to hold food down in a stomach that was used to complete emptiness. He repeatedly threw up the sumptuous canteen breakfast. He'd lost his lungs, he was searching for his posture, his connections, links, methods of breathing, dispersing the mental exercises that had kept him alive in the jungle but were now killing his brain. Every morning he opened his eyes and he was out there still. It was the beautiful Big Bertha nurse who saw his skeletons of men, their burning eyes alive, their sodomised hearts in tatters with sores and wounds. He twisted to Paddy. She, confronted by the atrocities of his crying, could not compare it to anything that she knew about or could help with.

Back Alive

When Frankie came back alive, everyone was surprised. In his twenty-fifth year, the priest stood over him and performed the last rites. They dragged him gently into camp and looked him over. He won't see morning, they said. He did see mornings for another twenty-five years. The day before his fiftieth birthday, he died. His daughter Eadie sat with him and he told her proudly that he had doubled his life expectancy.

"One more day," he'd said, "and that's enough."

The same priest came to the Repat and did it all over again. Frankie opened his eyes.

"It's him, Eadie," he whispered, "the same one," and he smiled a last soaring smile. Eadie blubbered and smiled with her father, but he'd already flown and she felt stupid.

Everyone left the ward and shook their heads. What a useless life, was the verdict. Eadie knew better.

When he returned to his mother's house after eighteen months at the Repat Hospital, he was full of the idea of recovery. He had been reading books, devouring all he could get, especially since Paddy had deserted him. The thin murmur of life, the brooding hush of jungle, the reveries and impulses of his youth, this was what was left to use to restore himself. He left the hospital sinewy, armed with an intricate map of survival. He arrived at the old gate, leaning inward. The street was in a state of lawlessness. Children with old faces sat on the gutter outside the milk bar. Some he knew, faces melted into familiar grins, spoke in chorus, tuneful voices, and ones that were out of kilter. They followed him up the street swaggering, asking how many of the bludgers he'd knocked off. Lovely young girls in predatory fashion followed at the rear. At the gate were bullies with looks that one shrank from. He grinned at the one who was aware of the terror he inspired. Frankie started a conversation with him about the tsetse fly, he showed his assassin teeth, the boy smiled as venomously as he could.

Frankie Wilt had them all laughing. Everything he said was barely permissible, hardly believable. In a masterful way he broke the floodgates, the dirtiness, the stink of the filthy war that sent him home, a sack of guts and on all fronts more like his captors than even he knew. He only wanted to eat rice, sit cross-legged and crouch. His two eyes slanted and rested in the sockets of his stretched face. His hair was shorn and he still gave off the smell of shit and ashes, clipped of the boisterous odours of dying. The scent of his boarded-up body could ruffle a mother. The narcotic network of ritual that he had lived in the jungle was still with him. He stood at his mother's front gate. He quickstepped up the path, his heart in his mouth.

He was not among the dead, not a front-page story, no glorious epitaph. He carried the war, flickering in the back of his mind. He wasn't new any more, he didn't work, not his bowels, nor his enthusiasm.

When Frankie Wilt came home from the war, on the sleepout door there was painted a swastika. Frankie only knew vaguely what it was. The boys from the street had done it; there was one on Max's at number seven, on her front door. That one caused more concern because Max knew more about being a Jew than the Wilt household. Alice had her eye on the culprit. Unfortunately it was the boy she liked best. Of the dozens that gathered under the streetlight and made her fence collapse, it had to be the one she liked best; the cheeky one that challenged her and answered back. He didn't know what he'd drawn either, he'd seen it in the *Argus* newspaper. He knew that you could flash it at Jews, if you knew any, and that it scared the piss out of them. He went over the fences with some housepaint he'd nicked from his dad and did the daring thing. Real quick before the lights in the backs of the houses came on and some old dad got hold of you.

The deed did not cause the stir that he'd hoped for. Max repainted her door quickly: no one much got to see his handiwork. Alice Wilt forgot about it, and it stayed there for a long time. If old Grandma Weinberg had seen it, she would have had a turn, but she stayed in the house now and away from the bungalow.

Frankie Wilt made it his business to find out what

it meant from the many books he was reading. He had taken up residence in the sleepout, and every book imaginable found its way there.

He had not been eager to say goodbye to the nurse. The men on the ward rested in peace, eating rhubarb and custard every night, spoonfed by galaxies of white nurses, holy bosses of the ward. Folding diapers for the men, dead tired girls with big hearts giving them a shove into the best of all possible worlds.

When Frankie lost one lung, he decided to take on his own cure. He asked the trolley ladies for special books and made lists of how his life could advance now that he could no longer be Fast-bowling Frankie. No one noticed his resistance to certain treatments. They were pleased that he went home early.

He spent some weeks hanging around his mother, little Alice Wilt, larger than the sky. She was still cheap labour at the knitting mills, running the whole factory, designing and ordering fabrics, shielding her girls from the sexual advances of the greedy boss and his mirror-image sons; speaking up for the women when they were underpaid and overworked. She knew when to lower hemlines or have buttons added to the cardigan pockets. She drew out the designs, made the patterns, organised loading and distribution, interviewed clients and buyers from the big department stores. In thirty years, she had one pay-rise and that was when she thought she might take long-service leave and the boss saw the factory rumble at the very thought. He gave her a raise. Ten pounds more! It was bloody unheard of, said the trade, but this was a problem of theological proportions. She was worth her weight in gold, he told his sons. Being not at all knowing, they replied, "Bullshit, Dad, everyone is expendable!" He gave her a week's leave while they thought about it.

Things went wrong almost immediately. The coherence of the floor was gone. Sixty per cent of the women did not speak English. It was impossible for the men to assert themselves. The women shrugged and turned off the machinery. By the third day, quotas had dropped; by Thursday many stayed home "sick" and a general walkout was menacing the whole buttonholing section. They refused to eyelet the waisted jackets because they all knew that Alice had planned a wrap-around. Alice was called back and, with her ten added pounds, felt prosperous. It took more than a month to get everything shipshape at the mills. The women had enjoyed their rebellion, it was hard to give up.

When Frankie came home, the Wilt sisters sang in the kitchen, after the roast, on Sunday afternoon; the banjos, zithers, ukuleles, mandolins and other hybrids were pulled out from under Alice's bed and they tuned up over a beer. Frankie looked at Grandma Weinberg who was pretty damn old; she would be ninety in a couple of months. She sat next to a bundle of samples that Alice had brought home from the factory. She was counting them, classifying them according to colour or feel.

"Moire, tapestry, weavestraw, terrycloth, apple green, mottled black, ultramarine blue, sienna brown, speckled like a trout, time is passing."

He listened to her say all this under her breath. What an eccentric old bugger, he thought. She looked across at him, then, their minds acrobatically lucid to each other. She smiled the grandmother's smile. As a boy he had liked this woman, his grandmother. Her erect, angry, funny, sentimental self tickled the havoc in him.

He visited his mother at work, a mad rage of rags under the needle, virgin wools, a mass of grey steel, giant needles and treadles all beating out a rhythm. He was the only man they welcomed on the floor, and he went there every day for months and ate lunch with his mother. He listened to the snick! snack! of needles going up and down. They sat out on the street with sandwiches and flasks at lunchtime. Away from the electrical charge and the dust of the cutting, they finished their coffee and garlic sausage. The other women hugged him because he was Alice's boy and he knew where he belonged.

At night at the dinner table, they talked shop. Even Grandma Weinberg, lost to the acceptable standards of bourgeois conversation, joined in with some trace of wisdom and understanding. They talked of little Eadie, the wandering grandchild, and they sang songs. "You sing this," said Alice, "you sing that." She sang a different part for each person, her voice changing to suit the tenors, the altos, the sopranos.

Then, with a triumphant sigh and a lifting of her little hands, "Now all sing together!"

The room filled with the lulling magic of harmonic trill. It ran along the length of the spine and took you to the great blue yonder. Melodies somersaulted, the seven sorrows buried in E-minor. Alice, for an hour, forgot the garment industry. To Frankie, it was like a shot of morphine. He felt lost in ecstatic space.

Some time passed before Frankie began disappearing for days at a time, into the sleepout, bolting the door from the inside. Every so often, he came out to walk the streets in his big winter overcoat, to exercise his lungs. No one noticed that he coughed blood, that breathlessness stopped him from joining the singalongs.

He went to the paint shop and bought cadmium yellows and mandarin blues and zinc white and sable-hair brushes. He collected house paints and watercolours, glues and varnishes. He sat in the park crosslegged, his eyes closed, his knees bent outward touching the wet ground. He taught himself to breathe from the stomach and he frequented the Chinese herbalist and the Turkish steam bath.

He was looking for a life and a cure.

"If you have tears," Alice Wilt told her children, "shed them now."

It was the same thing she told her son when she saw him drained, preparing to die at twenty-something. Though the doctors called her to the garden room at the hospital and remarked on his dissipated energies, she could see he would manage well enough on one lung and the radiance he had left.

"He could relapse at any time, you may not have him for long," they told her.

She did not rear up or square her shoulders. These men lived in a world without options. Perhaps without the constraints of rampant well-being, he may change into something else. From this time, his priority was inner liberty. Pity played no part in the scheme of things.

Alice saw nothing wrong with her faded son. Wrongness was not something she concentrated on for its own sake. Frankie for a long time now had not eaten with the family. He made lists of strange foods and brought them home decently wrapped in their brown paper parcels. There were big sunflowers along the wall of the sleepout. He had planted the seeds and urinated on them and they were blessed and nodding all around his abode. By candlelight at night, practising his breathing exercises, he fed his interest in theosophical and mystical literature given to him by Eunice, the Scotswoman he had met at the Turkish baths.

After he met Eunice, a broguey lass whose beauty stabbed at the heart and plumaged your secrets with her cooing, the hermetic order of his life became more tongue-in-cheek.

Eunice was a tall girl, lithe, with black curly hair. She travelled with three Scottish terriers and she earned a lucrative living as a snake dancer at the

Tivoli. Her eyes were challenging and feline, she was cat-like all over. As their friendship grew, he was to discover that she had her snakes close at hand at all times.

A long time passed before he would be enthusiastic enough to realise he wanted to do all kinds of terrible things with Eunice. At this time, he was still burning poems that he had written to Paddy. He would arrive at the Turkish baths in his soft felt hat, and Eunice would be curled up on the blue seat and look up as he entered. "And how is my wandering boy tonight?" she said in her thick Scottish accent. The dogs would all waddle towards him, their little stocky bodies lost against the dark carpet. He took the lavish towels she offered him and sat in the steam room. The angry red scar lashed down his torso. The jungle returned. Stormy visions bit into his senses.

When Alice Wilt first saw this scar, she got worked up. If Alice Wilt got worked up about anything, it was young boys going to war. When her son had told her that he was enlisting, she had frowned uncharacteristically and Frankie for the first time had felt her wrath. She knew wars: her father had fought in the first one. When radio broadcasts by Churchill and others lisped on about the heroics of might, she swore. She believed wholeheartedly in simple diversionary tactics, this distinctive woman. The benefits of knighthood for her blossoming boy would never be evident to her, she said. Cannon fodder was what she knew, the demand for fresh young boys to experiment with, to widen the horizons and vignettes of battle strategy. Her blood pressure rose dangerously and her swearing grew truly foul and ruthless – she had all the mothers worked up. Her usual shy domestic reserve offset an awesome drive, she felt that she could break her son's legs in order to prevent him from wasting his sweetness. The men told her, "You don't understand, Alice, we must fight, it's not as simple as you imagine." "As if I was a moron," she told Max from number seven.

Later, when people listened to the radio and got excited about night attacks and artillery bombardment, her son was already suffering the severance of ordinary human contact. The first bright arterial haemorrhage had occured and each night he had a hectic realisation of the inevitability of his own dying. Once he had gone off, Alice prepared for his return, the mending that would take place. She got on with her life and ceased her ranting and thought of other things.

Years later, when just about everyone was dead, not least of all Frankie Wilt, Alice helped her granddaughter, Eadie, to hide young men from conscription to the Vietnam War. Eadie would inherit the same prejudices as her granny. Alice, who had the street children leaning on her fence, would later play cards with young fugitives for days in her back room. They would steal money from her purse to buy marijuana. They chopped her wood and painted the lounge room in the peach colour that she had wanted for twenty years. They were trouble, but at least they didn't go to war, and she was pleased with herself for making an effort.

When Frankie lived in the sleepout, he often disappeared for months. He left a note and went away. A couple of times baby Eadie Wilt came with one of the aunties who was on a visit to the city. When she was two, for instance, Alice took her to the zoo, and they went to look at the Christmas windows at the Myer department store. Frankie Wilt was not home and was very depressed when he heard that Eadie had come and gone. Eadie herself said she could not remember her dad before the day he appeared, out of the blue, at the school gate. He walked her home and stayed at the hotel for a week or so. The aunties said he was a charmer. Paddy said he was wicked. Siddy Church told Eadie that it amounted to the same thing.

A Girl as Loud as the Sky

Years rolled by, and the baby Eadie stayed firmly buffeted by stout grandmothers. She was influenced by both of them. At a certain age, she discovered that life's luck had an eloquent way of balancing out the glories, all the truths that for a certain child-time you actually believed. The truths of the beloved grannies began to be a rickety fortress and, lo and behold, the grace of the black-browed mother contained a prose of exquisitely hidden virtue. Eadie Wilt, in monitoring the genetic diversity in her family, began to savour the originality of her mother. As the general family horizon broadened and she knew her father and other grandmother, she grew sure that looking into people's truth, you'd be sure to find something else. A terrible upsidedownness that she'd never noticed before.

She was visiting her father. They were at the beach with seagulls crying above the swoosh of the waves. She read over his shoulder, her brown-child's arms around his neck. "A girl has come to stay in our house, a girl as loud as the sky." He took her by her ear handles and flipped her over his shoulder. He could do magic like that, this wicked charmer dad.

On the beach with them was the Scottish girl

Eunice, who months back had flirted with Frankie Wilt at the Turkish baths. She was often there with Frankie when Eadie made her visits to the Wilt household.

That morning, they had set out early in Frankie's old Vauxhall. Eunice's three scottie dogs sat identically square and black with tartan collars on tartan blankets in the back seat. In the boot, placed in an open picnic basket, were Eunice's snakes. Eadie had been to the Tivoli one Saturday matinee to see Eunice perform with her pets. Eadie thought it was the best thing she had ever seen. She liked Eunice, the purr of her voice and the words she used: "wee lass" and "bonny laddy" and trashy things like that.

"Eunice had no clothes on except a pair of undies," she later told her Grandma Alice Wilt. The snakes wrapped all around her body and Eunice wore a blonde wig. A jungle of naked cupids filled the stage, and the giant snake flipped to the ground and vanished into a corner and everyone screamed. Then the cupids danced with their undies on and Eunice lurked in the middle while they covered her in feathers and then she dropped down and died. They were in the last row of the topmost gallery and Eadie was very excited and ran down the stairs knowing exactly what she wanted to be when she grew up. In the foyer a very large photograph of Eunice stood. "Now Showing!" it said, and you could see how black the snake was and how big Eunice's tits were.

She told all of this to Grandma Alice. Hanging

around the dressing-room with Eunice, she soon held the snakes and knew they were harmless. She listened to the women.

"Everyone talks about their tits there," she told Alice Wilt.

"Yes," said Alice Wilt, "but it's better to keep them where they can't be seen."

"Summers are lovely," said Eunice, as she cuddled Eadie up and down and pulled the skirt of her woollen bathers down over her mound. The seagulls squabbled and the scotties all stood and sniffed and gruffly lay down again in different positions. They all reeked of coconut oil, and Eadie hitched her saggy bathers and sand dropped out onto her sunburnt feet. They packed the car and Eunice sailed into an aria. The snakes were put in the boot but they had long ago discovered an opening in the underfelt lining of the boot. They could snake along and come into the cabin of the car and position themselves above their mistress. She stroked and rubbed the bumps in the felt lining of the Vauxhall. Eunice was still singing heartily; the sun went down and Eadie, dead-tired in the back with the scotties, knew there would never be a better day.

Early on Sunday mornings, Eunice would grab her out of bed before the sun came up. Sometimes there was even a mist. She would dress her in her jodhpurs and they would go to the stables behind the old bakery and hire two horses. Then they would canter around the Shrine of Remembrance on the tanbark edging the big park. Occasionally, the big horses would break into a gallop and little Eadie would feel the quiet morning erupt and her small heart pound with shock. The mystery was the thundering joy she felt at being so scared. Eunice would grab the reins, cooing and calming with her secret lisps. Sometimes they would visit Eunice's father on the way home, at the Turkish baths in High Street. The heavy dark curtains with fringes gave off a breath of dust if you touched them. Later in life, if Eadie went to the gym and sat in the steam room, she always thought of this dark place with its hint of brothel.

Eunice's father smoked little black cigarettes. He strained away at puffing on them in a compelling manner all through their visit. Eunice would play the piano and her old father told Eadie stories.

"The day before Mozart died, his friends gathered around his bed and they sang a Requiem. Mozart sang the alto part. Mozart sang a few bars then burst into tears."

Eadie saw tears in Eunice's father's eyes. She thought Mozart must have been his good friend. She patted him on the back as her grandmother did when she cried.

"He did not leave many belongings," he told Eadie. "A billard table, a piano, a mouse-coloured overcoat and eighteen pocket handkerchiefs."

"Why did he die so young?"

"It was the eighteenth century. People shat in the street and rotten meat was simply spiced with pepper.

Women routinely had ten children and expected that at least half would die. Mozart already had had smallpox, typhoid fever, rheumatic fever, pneumonia and numerous abcesses and recurrent fevers."

Eadie looked shocked. Eadie went home with the heroic possibilites of E-flat firmly implanted in her baby brain. Marvellous new words assembled themselves in her speech; preludes and quintets, serenades and exotic harmonies. It was Mozart that Eunice was playing on the piano, Eadie was told. He went to a glass-doored cupboard and brought out a heavy mud-coloured album, a treasure! It said, "A Victor Musical Masterpiece." He put it on his gramophone.

"Mozart's Twenty-seventh Concerto in B-Flat."

At this point, Eadie wanted to go home. She knew that her grandmother would be taking the roast out of the oven. All her grannie's sisters and her cousins would be arriving for the Sunday roast. On Sundays, at lunchtime, Alice Wilt's sisters and all the cousins would come. After the roast dinner was eaten, Alice sent the children for the instruments. Under her bed were the zithers and mandolins, ukeleles, guitars, next to the white pot she used for night-time pissing.

On the bench, they all sat and, one by one, Alice would go down the line: "This is what you sing," and, "Eadie, sing exactly this."

Next, she would show the chords. She would push small fingers down on the strings. Eadie picked it up quickly. She was the favourite. At night-time, she slept in her grannie's bed after Pop died. She was there when Pop died, she could relate every detail. She believed that he'd eaten one too many Cadbury chocolate bars. That night she had walked to the milk bar with Alice and bought him his usual Cherry Ripe and the large Cadbury milk chocolate block. He ate them in bed. The wrappers were still on his belly when Alice looked in to turn off the bedside lamp. He was dead. Alice thought he looked so calm and peaceful that she called Eadie in to look. He was still very warm and Eadie took his hand and they had a conversation and Alice wiped the chocolate crumbs from his mouth and had a bit of a cry.

When Eadie Wilt went home again, her mother, Paddy, lost all patience with her talk of tits and girls loud as the sky. Even more infuriating was the Scottish accent that she had acquired, and dancing in her undies with a provocative leer and trilling endlessly, day and night. Her biggest secret of all was playing with Nilli, the girl of Max from number seven. Eadie was in love with Nilli on the second visit to her granny's. Alice took her there and the two girls warily surveyed each other for peculiarities and codes of girlhood that fuelled their ardours. She took Nilli to her father's sleepout. Everyone liked it because it was weird. Just a plain old sleepout like everyone had from the outside, but when you opened the door and stepped inside, well! It was the jungle. The light socket was strangled by vines and foliage. You instantly felt steamy and wanted to take off your cardigan. This room was suffocating, like the first time you entered the river caves at Luna Park. Not one inch of the room was left unpainted. It was Frankie Wilt's post-war therapy and his first painting exercise. More than witty paint effects, it was too nightmarish to be habitable; perhaps that's why her father was always away. In the leaves you could always find something you hadn't seen before. *Trompe l'œil* chickens and tiny black-eyed men with their mouths open wide and grinning. Women in triangle hats balancing tumblers on their heads, and cages of men.

"Wanna play doctors?" asked Nilli of Eadie. The sleepout interested her only because she had been born there. They both had been told of the labours that brought Nilli into the world.

"What's doctors?" asked Eadie.

She was jealous of the stories of Nilli's miraculous birth. They walked past Eunice sunbaking on the lawn near the passionfruit vine. By the time they had negotiated Alice Wilt's decaying fence and front gate and made their way to Nilli's house, they had forgotten about the doctors game. Nilli's mother Max was baking. Every Friday she made twists of pastry, light and melting, covered with powdered icing sugar. She called the girls and handed them a whole plate of these twists, just cooling. Nilli took them and the girls sauntered into the back yard, jamming the pastries into their mouths with pixie fingers. They went into the lavatory and put the plate on the wooden plank seat. It was cool and shady in this place. Cracks of light came in, but the sun was locked out.

Nilli hated the sun. She was pudding-white with her great round face capped by a circle of very black hair, bobbed carefully by Max. The plate was yellow, which was a subject good enough for conversation.

"I hate yellow," said Nilli.

"Me, too," said Eadie, wise enough to know that she was not the leader in this game.

"Jews wear yellow stripes and yellow stars," said Nilli. "Then, after they do that, then, everybody kills them."

Eadie felt uncomfortable with this and wanted to go home. It was almost as bad as Mozart, and she was feeling a bit sick from all the sugar. Nilli, feeling the change in spirit, changed the subject.

"Wanna play doctors?"

"What's doctors?"

So the friendship was saved for the day, and Eadie took off her dress and undies and stood in the dark lav with her singlet on.

"You take yours off too," she said to Nilli.

"No! I don't have to, I'm the doctor!" answered the dark brat with her face full of icing sugar.

"Oh! Well, what do I do now?" asked Eadie not too curious. Nilli tried hard to think what the boy from Hebrew school on Saturdays had told her about this game. Improvisation being the key to all original creation, she firmly took the narrative.

"First, you must hold this piece of toilet paper in your bum."

She held up a strip of toilet paper and carefully

folded a border around the four sides. Then she held it near Eadie's crack and willed her to grasp the paper with her cheeks. With all her might, determination and willpower, Eadie tried to do this, but she succeeded only in feeling the lump come down that told you you needed to go.

"This is stupid," she told Nilli, climbing on the lav and pulling the rude face you did when you wanted to do it. Just then, Max opened the door.

"Finished with the plate, girls?" she asked. "Don't take food in the lavatory," said Max to Nilli. Eadie already knew that food in the lav was taboo.

As a middle-aged woman, Eadie met a man briefly in a crowd.

"We've met," he said. "I'm Nilli's brother."

For the life of her, Eadie could not remember her childhood flame's brother.

"She always talked about you," he said.

"Where is she now?" said Eadie, already planning a meeting.

"Oh, she killed herself when she was nineteen," he said.

Eadie had for many years imagined, from time to time, what Nilli would be like. At twenty-five and at forty. She was startled to know that she had given up such a long time ago. Eunice also disappeared. On one visit Eadie looked for a sign of her but she was gone. Her father was not in the sleepout.

"He lives on a beach in a caravan," Grandma Alice

told her grand-daughter. One day Eadie saw Eunice in *Woman's Day*. She was very old and her tits were somewhere where they couldn't be seen. Eadie smiled to herself and tried to sail into the aria that Eunice always hummed. She now owned a reptile farm in Perth and had married a Scotsman who loved terriers. Not a trace of the young Eunice was there in that picture, just the name and the snakes and the associations. Somewhere inside her, Eadie still wanted to be a snake-dancer at the Tiv, even after everyone was dead or old and the building had been pulled down.

Our Own Sex

When young Eadie stayed with her Grandma Alice, she slept in her bed. That is, of course, after all others with claims to this comfortable and commendable place had died. Old great-grandma had slept with Alice for several years. She regularly hauled herself onto the windowsill and pissed out of the window and everybody talked about it. She died in the bed. It was a popular bed for dying.

Now Eadie slept there. They went to the library with the card and exchanged books. They went to bed together after a bath in the old laundry smelling of baby powder and wearing their long, rained-on pink nighties. They propped up the pillows and settled in for a good read. Alice read aloud, sometimes very fast, almost falling asleep, reviving with a jolt. She told Eadie she preferred books written by our own sex.

"Books written by women, there's less of them," she commented, "After a while you've read everything at the library and you have to look really hard."

Alice preferred books that made you get a lump in your throat. The current one had a plot that began with two parents being killed by a falling tree and the only child, suddenly an orphan, sets out to find her grandmother's house which is situated in another state two-hundred-and-fifty miles away. After weeks of near-starvation and exposure, she arrives, two hundred pages of adventure later, at the gate of her grandmother. She has come through snow (which Eadie had never seen) and a freak blizzard with a hessian bag wrapped around her. She stumbles to the cabin and manages a scratching on the door. The grandmother opens it as the child drops down in the snow with her last wan smile on her poor wasted face.

Both Alice and Eadie were severely troubled by this ending. They held back angry sobs of frustration. They fell into an exhausted sleep, consoling themselves by holding each other tightly and sobbing brokenly until Alice's snoring excluded all other considerations.

If they didn't get to the library in time to find children's books, then Alice would read *Jane Eyre* again. Eadie got to know the opening lines very well and they gave her a good feeling:

"There was no possibility of taking a walk that day. We had been wandering, indeed, in the leafless shrubbery an hour in the morning; . . . the cold winter wind had brought with it clouds so sombre, and a rain so penetrating, that further outdoor exercise was now out of the question."

This reminded Eadie of the flood she had been lost in. She knew about penetrating rain and sombre clouds. She thought that if she could not be a snake-dancer at the Tivoli, she would write sombre and penetrating stories. She wrote small ones for her grandmother and used every big, beautiful, penetrating and sombre word she had ever heard. Alice said they were very good.

"Don't overdo it, darling."

This was much the same thing that her other grandmother had told her. She knew that they both liked her stories, though. She was of our own sex and that counted for something in this family. Alice always pushed to get to Chapter 26 in *Jane Eyre*:

"Sophie came at seven to dress me: she was very long indeed in accomplishing her task; so long that Mr Rochester, grown, I suppose, impatient of my delay, sent up to ask why I did not come."

This was Alice Wilt's favourite chapter, and her voice rang out stridently. Eadie didn't like the ending but she was happy to listen to the combinations of words: "damping humiliation" and "he hews down like a giant the prejudices of creed and caste that encumber it".

She wondered what it all meant. She suspected that Jane Eyre was well and truly overdoing it with her autobiography, but grandma Alice overlooked this because she was of our own sex.

There was much more to this *Jane Eyre* book, as Eadie would learn, a story within a story. Firstly, the front page said: "An autobiography edited by Currer Bell".

"That's not the truth," said Alice Wilt. "Charlotte Brontë wrote it and gave herself a pretend name, Currer Bell, because she probably thought a manly-sounding name would be more helpful in having it published."

There were many questions of What? and Why? and Who did what in 1847 in a house called Haworth? In an episodic way, a story that Eadie liked much better came out, told simply by her grandmother.

"There were five sisters and one brother: Elizabeth, Maria, Charlotte, Emily, Anne, brother Branwell. Their mother died and they lived in isolation with their father, Patrick. Soon the children all began to die, even Charlotte. They invented characters, wrote fables, fantasies, poems, journals. They invented a country, Angria. They had a servant, Tabby, who remained at the parsonage for thirty years. She had known the countryside when it was frequented by fairies but she said it was the factories that drove them away."

Eadie was excited; she always looked for the stories behind the story from then on. All her life, she sought out and studied closely the work written by our own sex. In the workbook that she kept in the sleepout at Grandma Alice's, she wrote out the words "disenchanted stoicism, inexpressible sadness". Eadie wrote down the words that Jane Eyre had written about her own marriage: "To be together is for us to be at once as free as in solitude, as gay as in company."

She also knew the horrible truth, that Charlotte Brontë died of excessive morning sickness. To find out what that was, why one would die from it, filled Eadie's whole holiday at Grandma Alice's. All Charlotte's sisters and her brother had a cough, just like Eadie's father, and they died young and, it seemed, very easily. Eadie had read *Wuthering Heights* and cried so much that Alice had to get up and make some custard and they sat up at the Laminex table in the kitchen trying to undo the damage. It was too late for that, Eadie had already uncovered all the connections, she knew that *Jane Eyre* had been a great success and that *Wuthering Heights* was rejected and that Emily Brontë had died in the year after.

Eadie dreamt of having brothers and sisters, as many as Charlotte Brontë. Her only experience of this sort of play was down by the river with the lake-tribe kids. They made her eat dirt and tied her to a tree and even one day made a fire at her feet, of matchsticks. It went out as her mother called down the hill from the backstairs. Eadie was untied, and scrambled up the muddy hill. Paddy looked baffled, concerned with tea-tables and the indisputable fact of her ferocious, yapping child blundering up the backstairs. Eadie had developed a sneer, the black art of doing what she liked. Savage and hardy, and always missing. Alice Wilt read Catherine and Heathcliff, skipping over the bits she thought too delicate. The fairytale of *Wuthering Heights* and Thrushcross

Grange and all those sisters coughing and Branwell drinking himself to death were forces that interlocked with her own grandmother's magic. Alice Wilt had a feverish belief in the occult, and spoke to all sorts of dead people through cards and an upside-down glass that walked up and down letters and spelt out messages. Alice's optimistic belief in the spirits eventually made Eadie a believer. All sorts of omens showed themselves to the keenly observant child.

Paddy complained that every time Eadie came back from the Wilts', she was strange. Sometimes her father would be there, and he would teach her all sorts of useful things like how to draw Mickey Mouse in one line without lifting the pencil from the paper. Or how to copy, upside-down, someone else's signature. Paddy did not like the sound of that at all and made a phone call to Alice Wilt to complain. After all, Frankie Wilt had been in trouble for that sort of thing. She heard her mother explaining her fears to Grandma Alice. Sometimes she would interrupt politely and say something like: "If you want to start a fire, you've got to strike a match." But Paddy didn't take to that at all. Alice Wilt told Eadie, "Most people will agree with you, if you just keep quiet," or "When you talk you can only say something that you already know; when you listen, you may learn what someone else knows."

One day, in the sleepout, Eadie read Hemingway. Ernest Hemingway, it said, and had bloody bulls on the cover.

"A bully," announced Alice Wilt, "who liked to kill small animals! No great achievement there."

She scoffed. Alice bundled Eadie up and off they went in Alice's car to a band practice.

"It's a novelty band," said the manager of Legget's Ballroom just around the corner from Alice's house in St Edmonds Rd.

"I don't know if we can hire you. An all-women band has a limited appeal. What else do you do?"

"What do you mean?" asked Alice. "We are playing our instruments. Do you want us to wait on tables or sweep the floor as well?"

"We'll call you," he joked and Eadie pulled a hate face at him from her place on the carpet. She already knew she was not an adorable child. He didn't bother to pinch her cheek. Alice's band played anyway. In the park where the Salvation Army band usually stood on Sunday morning. It was a great success and the pigeons shat themselves on sandwich lunches, and rich and varied interweavings of people drifted through the park. The children ran wild. Eadie Wilt and her ten cousins ate fairy floss and got overexcited and everyone got a smack except Eadie. Aunt Nancy came over to the children, every now and then, to say "Stop showing off," or "Wait till we get home." Eadie's home was a long way off in the big old hotel, and she could show off as much as she liked. Her Auntie felt like she could wipe that sneer right off her face but she didn't dare because everyone knew that Eadie was Alice Wilt's favourite. That night in bed they read *Robinson Crusoe* and the Brontës faded into childhood. Eadie forgot about dark intentions. Angels and monsters, nuns and witches engaged in elaborate dialogue in her daydreams but they all became less morbid. She grew more inclined to wish-fulfilment and drawing Mickey Mouse in one line.

She was put tearfully on the train early one morning to go home. Someone was in charge of her, it was Auntie Ruth who worked in the dining car. The train made twenty-six stops and these rides were to instil a love of trains in her forever.

"I could live on a train," she said, as she made her way from Calcutta to Trivandrum years later. It didn't matter how long the journey took. She felt as if she had arrived.

She had conversations with families and told great big whopping lies to other people's mothers, ones that would never have worked on hers. Once she was sitting all alone watching sheep, mile after mile of sheep, a man came in and sat beside her and tried to talk. "Would you like to come to the dining car for a lemonade?" he asked.

"I can't," she told him, "I'm just little."

"I think he was a deviant," she told Grandma Siddy when she got home, getting the word just right.

The luck of life was very clear. She was going to have a great and wonderful life. She thought about this often. On the train when the boys came through, being rude and slashing seats, she smiled at them.

More than one mother commented on the strangeness of that. "See things from the other person's point of view," that was what Grandma Siddy always said.

Next day, after she had been made a fuss of, and Paddy had cuddled her a lot and asked questions about the Wilts, she settled into looking with new eyes at her reality. Log fires crackled in the rooms, the aunties played darts and billiards. Grandma Siddy was polishing glasses and talking to the policeman. He had a pot before him. The beer was amber and cold but he was not enjoying it. Siddy, still polishing, held a glass to the light and rubbed. "If I had my way, I wouldn't let any men in here at all," she said. He smiled.

"But since by law I have to, I'm letting them all in, makes no difference to me."

He kept smiling, sipped a little into the froth and had to wipe his mouth because he looked silly with his top lip all frothed up. Eadie climbed up on the stool beside him and, leaning on her forearms, studied him closely. He was considering things. He was scared of Siddy. She could be tough but everything kept spilling over into poetry and he didn't know what to bloody do then.

He decided to go with "the Law" since she brought it up. Eadie noticed he had tennis shoes on with his blue uniform and she was shocked. "Anarchy" was the word she thought of – so newly learnt, this word, and she saw it everywhere. In the meantime, the two pursued the subject of the law.

"Mrs Church, it *is* against the law to allow

Aboriginals into this hotel."

"Correction," said Siddy, "I can let whomever I bloody-well please into my establishment and the law is about selling them alcohol and you'll get no one saying I do that! Ask them."

The gun jammed! He looked over to the billiard table where Imlay, a very large black lady, was enjoying a lager with the aunties.

"My guest," anticipated Siddy, placing the sparkling glass on the shelf behind the bar. He leaned back, reloaded.

"Not that I would ever go that far, but this could close you down."

This was a home-made bomb as far as Siddy was concerned. She herself had a huge collection of weapons, but she categorised this encounter as not worth any effort.

"Drink up," she said to him, "and I'll call 'Lalla' over for a yarn."

Imlay glanced imperially across the drinkers, having picked up her pet name. He drank up and moved from the stool. As he made his way to the doors, he saw that every second face was black. It was worse than he thought.

While all this official business was going on in the front bar, the kitchen was caught in the current of Siddy's New Years resolution.

"Opposition from others is often proof that you're on the right track," she told Eadie.

Secret Hidings & Women's Business

Eadie liked Imlay. She had come with Iris and Rose, the bookie's wife. They had banged on the front doors one night after midnight and toppled headfirst into the front parlour. Siddy let them in after raging down the stairs cursing at the racket.

The whole house was up. The cryings were so suggestive of final and desolate sorrow that all doors opened and aunties swarmed the stairs. Their feet stomped along the landing. The whole house shook. Eadie shuddered out of sleep as all the lights came on. She made the pilgrimage downstairs, but she was shoved to one side by the hostile aunties making ready for battle.

The voices were shocked, hushed to a whisper.

"Who did this?" whispered Siddy.

Imlay bled. They carried her to the big table and laid her down there. They tried to lift her dress but she held it down, determined and dry-eyed. The tapestry cloth was absorbing the blood. The women were pushing towels into her. Great masses of shivery liver, red and wobbly came out from between her legs. The table was overflowing with these jellymeats. The women moaned together. Everyone went for buckets. No one stood still except Eadie. She was wondering if this was dying or one of life's big events.

From outside came the doctor, sworn to secrecy. Bribed to come, reminded by Siddy of favours and borrowed monies. The doctor bent over the table and, with many "Jesus Christs" and "struths", he did what he did and left. When they noticed Eadie there, they bundled her off. They were cleaning up, wiping down and drinking morbidly to women's business which was all Imlay had to say when asked what bastard had done this.

This enactment of Eadie Wilt's most theatrical fears, ones she was only modestly aware of having, kept her awake this night and many others. She went to school next day with the horrors. The aunties all wore ferocious scowls that said too busy, and Siddy Church was nowhere to be seen.

There was no record of the night before. Maybe it was one of those hauntings that seem so spectacular at night, so mad and elaborate and enthralling. When she came home at three, the saloon bar was closed and the kitchen was under seige. Numerous men from the lake clustered around Siddy, pointing at her with long prodding fingers. Mantel, who was very much alive at that time, was all for calling the police, and Paddy agreed. Siddy would have none of it.

"Those women are not here!" she told them, and finally she took her huge bunch of keys from the pocket in her apron. She led the column of angry black men upstairs, to the rooms. Solemnly, she opened door after door.

"Not here . . . Not here . . . Not here."

By the time they left to go home, Siddy knew what had been done, by whom.

Siddy was standing at the bar folding serviettes. The men liked her. They had not drunk methylated spirits since she had taken them in, and they knew she challenged the law to have them there.

It was the 1950s. No one spoke about songlines, and if you knew your tribal name you did not tell it. Life was patchy, for the men. Ceremonial centres, once unfailing waterholes where, perhaps, the ancestors' footprints converged, could still be the place for what the white people called corroborees. Siddy was breaking taboos, the aunties said. Looking at the wrong man in the wrong way. Much later, when Mantel Bonlevi died her horrible death, the black men looked down at her feet and never met her eye again.

Eadie kept her ear to the ground. There was plenty of "sshh's" and "careful, she might hear you", but she saw that there was much activity and many comings and goings to and from the verandah. This balcony was Eadie's main playground, and she had been perfecting her backflips and splits on the old bedsprings that she used as a trampoline. Now she was all but banned from going out there. Some of the aunties always sat there now, just outside, guarding the doors. Supposedly shelling peas or folding laundry.

"Out of bounds, Eadie, love, keep out of the way, we're very busy, Eadie."

All the aunties knew where the women were and Eadie was catching on fast. They were in the old storerooms which did not have a doorway into the internal passage. In fact, you could not reach them from inside the house. They had been built as an afterthought on to the verandah itself and you had to walk around three sides of the balcony before you came upon them. The doors were always padlocked, and the rooms held all the discarded furniture and junk from the 1890s that had belonged to the owner-builder of this rambling place. All activities for several days centred on these rooms. Cupboards and old bathtubs obscured the existence of not only the lost rooms but the end of the verandah itself. Trays of steaming foods were convoyed up.

"A lot of people are out there, judging by all that mashed potato," said the cook who was as much in the dark as Eadie.

At the dinner table, the aunties made faces at each other over Eadie's head. She pretended to lose interest. From the board in the bar, she took the key to number eighteen which she knew was adjacent to the storerooms. She waited for the hour when the women would be settling downstairs for an end-of-the-day yarn. She could see the tops of their heads from the bannister on the landing. Everyone accounted for down there, she thought, good! She slipped into number eighteen. She didn't turn on the light. She put her ear to the wall and listened. Nothing at all. This room had another door that went into a bathroom, but it had been nailed shut. Instantly Eadie now saw that the persons in the storerooms were using this bathroom which once led on to the verandah but had been partitioned off for years. Eadie thrilled. It was like discovering secret rooms. Siddy must have nailed up this door and taken out the partitions so the bathroom could be used without coming into the house. She liked the slimy rat feeling she got when she spied through the crack. She was aided in her criminal acts by the fact that at this time Paddy had an admirer who regularly came to take her out. She stayed out till all hours. Sneaky Eadie used this time to explore the possibilities, for learning all that was none of her business. By the end of the week, she had been in the room every night. There was more light in the room in the afternoon and she saw a small window high in the wall on the verandah side. If she climbed on the wardrobe, she would be able to see through it. Not so easy! A chair on the table would do it but she couldn't risk the scraping sounds of furniture moving. She waited until after dinner, when all the aunties were settled on the couches with their shoes off. She ran down the passage in her socks and unlocked the door. Quickly she grabbed the pillows from the bed and put them under the back legs of the small table and pulled it towards the cupboard. She climbed on to the top of the cupboard by lifting the chair on to the table. They were heavy and she was forced to sneeze into her sleeve from the dust. She was working hard at these gymnastics. She saw the small window above her. She opened it and heard voices. She listened to the conversations for a long time, breathing shallow breaths; the cupboard rattled as she clung on. The light snapped off suddenly. Her heart was in her mouth. Two women's voices, a wistful conversation about going home. She crouched on that tall cupboard listening until it went quiet. The room was in pitch blackness. When she was lowering herself onto the chair, the dread thing happened. She missed and came crashing down. The light came on in the little window and someone moved around in the room. She was winded and her ankle hurt. She had the key, though, and the door opened quietly. With her hundred hearts pounding she ran a shaky, hopping run down the passage to her room and into her bed. She counted to ten before she heard anything. No one came to search. She did not look like a criminal. No surveillance of Eadie was arranged. Every night, every waking hour was spent at her stake-out point crouched on top of the cupboard.

In the room, there were many women and children. Imlay was on the bed and looked sick. She had bandages around her head and a sticky plaster on her naked breast. Eadie saw the nurse come and peel back the covers. She put something from a bottle onto Imlay's bum and Imlay cried out.

"It's healing up, Imlay."

"I wanna go home," wailed Imlay.

Just then, Siddy Church came in with trays of food that Eadie could smell.

"I heard that, Imlay," she said in a very gentle voice. "You're staying here till I get this all sorted out."

A great deal of laughter rose up and sounds of enjoyment. Siddy sat watching. Imlay, after several plates of roast beef, felt more invigorated.

"I'm going home tomorrow," she said in an unassailable tone. One of Siddy's virtues was that she didn't beat around the bush. "If I come up here and you've gone, I'll go to the police and register a complaint. It will say that your husband raped his niece, and when you tried to stop him, he forced a bottle into your backside and broke it in his efforts. He will go to jail and Rosie will be taken away and you'll never be able to come here again."

Eadie's saucer eyes widened in the shadows. The women went berserk, wailing low, and plates were thrown down. They cried and floundered and bumped into each other. They took to Siddy as well, shaking their fists at her, coming very close to her face and speaking wet garbled hisses and crying hoarsely. Siddy held her ground, cradling a couple of skinny girls. She looked so mournful that Eadie felt a great welting sob coming up from her chest. She pressed her fingers deep into her eye sockets to make the tears go away.

Eadie was shocked at her grandmother's blackmailing tactics. On the other hand, she did not understand why the women wanted to go home if terrible things happened to them there. She was so mixed up. Nightmares came and she cried a lot, but could not stop herself from climbing onto the wardrobe and hearing more. Every night Siddy Church was in there and Imlay told her again she was going home.

"You bin doing this! You peoples," she told Siddy.

"My peoples," said Siddy, "are the women. Women were forced here in chains. They sit here and they say 'This is not my land!' Women don't have a land. Your men sell you for cigarettes!"

The women became so angry with her, and the children grizzled and squirmed out of her lap.

It happened that, the next day, the locks were changed on the door of number eighteen. Eadie was not suspected of anything, she was just little. The security on the balcony doors eased up too. She found she could go out there all the way around and no one pulled her back.

She began asking questions. Then she was allowed among the black women. Even sleeping out there some nights was allowed. Paddy was glad to have a good night's sleep, a rest from the recurring nightmares that her daughter was having.

"How'd you get a sore bum, Imlay?"

"Who told you that, Eadie Wilt?"

Imlay didn't mind; the child was cheeky and you didn't know what she'd say next.

When Eadie Wilt grew up and said she was a

writer, she wrote stories that she said came a bit from this time, from Iris and Rosie and Imlay and all their ways.

No trouble was done with Eadie and the women until she saw some of the men at the back of the chook pen killing one of Siddy's chooks. They did not see her until she was standing right up against them and she scared them out of their wits.

"Are you killing one of Siddy's chickens?" she asked.

The men laughed a lot and held the chicken up and shook the bird.

"Siddy gave us this chicken," said the man who Eadie knew was Imlay's husband.

"My grannie knows about Imlay's sore bum," said Eadie, getting to the heart of the matter. If colour drained from the men's faces, Eadie could not tell; but they started looking funny and headed down the embankment to the river without another word, dropping the chicken at her feet.

She was never suspected, because of the fact of her being "just little", of any involvement in the affair. The very night when Eadie had seen the men with the chicken, the matter came to a head. "As matters have a way of doing," said Siddy.

Once the men were alerted to Siddy Church's ongoing interest in the affair, they began nosing around the hotel again. For a while, they had believed that the women had gone bush, but now they knew differently.

The women from the lost rooms had long ago stopped all caution. If anyone came to the back of the hotel, they would notice that on the second-floor verandah, a small uninhibited party was going on every night. The men stood in the bushes looking up to the verandah.

"Imlay?" hissed the man. "You there?"

Her head bobbed up and they caught sight of her and began to scale the verandah posts. The women hurled pot-plants and tipped beer on the men's heads.

The women had eased up on wanting to go home. Now they said, "Women have no land." They helped in the kitchen a bit and allowed themselves to be indoctrinated by Siddy.

"Bugger youse!" yelled Imlay and all the children were laughing and finally, the men coaxed them down. They slithered down the verandah posts. All the children went, even though the mothers tried to hold them. Next morning, there was no sign of anyone out there.

A few months later, Imlay came back.

"Where's my baby?" she asked Siddy.

"You lost that one," Siddy told her. "It came out before it was baked."

Imlay searched around the hotel anyway. Then she went upstairs to listen to little Eadie Wilt tell some whoppers.

"Once I lost a baby and they sat me on the lav," Imlay told Eadie, who was still only little, "and it came out and they flushed it down."

Eadie was impressed. She'd never been lied to like that before.

After the flood and Eadie's disappearance, Willy Howe came to live with Siddy Church and the aunties. There was a lady who could tell stories, thought Eadie. She loved Willy Howe and Imlay. Sometimes she thought that her stories were almost as good.

Being Schooled

At school, Eadie Wilt asked the teacher: "Where are all the women? Didn't they do anything, go anywhere?"

It was not enough that the class reader said, "Betty can jump". She was already listening to *Jane Eyre* at Grandma Alice's and she knew that babies got flushed down toilets if they were black. At her house, the women did it all but in the *Famous Five*, the girls tagged along.

"Don't be difficult, Eadie Wilt," the teacher told her.

Her knees scabbed, her nose bled, and the teacher was driven to distraction and made the big mistake of smacking the horrible child. Eadie ran out of the classroom and climbed a tree. She would not come down. She had learnt the black art of saying no. The headmaster came, the sports teacher came. Playtime passed, lunchtime and hometime all went by. Eadie was feeling smug as she waited in her tree. The whole school assembled below. Actually, it was more like the whole town, since word had got around. She had it all worked out. Siddy would come, Grandma Siddy, and she would stand down here and say, "Why are you up a tree Eadie?"

And Eadie would answer, "I was smacked."

"By whom?" Siddy would ask, and Eadie would not say, but the teacher would own up and Siddy would glare at the teacher and scare the piss out of her. Now, Eadie was smacked by Paddy, her mum, and thrown against walls and lifted by her hair, but that was different! Grandma Siddy and the aunties were working on that. There was something wrong with Paddy. She only went like that when she had been drinking, and Siddy was on constant alert and the aunties were always sweeping in and carrying Eadie to safety. Sometimes their timing was off and Eadie copped it bad.

"Grandmothers hate to see their babies hurt," Siddy told Eadie. She suffered when Paddy hit Eadie.

"And then a bloody stranger hits her! Well, that's another matter!" Siddy's looks were really impressive. Eadie could not wait until she arrived.

Her expectations were not satisfied that day because her grandmother did not come, nor her mother nor any of the aunties. She felt weakened when she saw that they had sent Paddy's new beau. Eadie shrank as she saw him drive up to the school fence. He was Reggie Spicer. He had red hair. A hank of the greasy stuff flopped over one eye and he was constantly raising his great white freckled hand to his head to flip it back. Eadie watched with fascination whenever he did this. He did it three times as he left his car and made his way through the small crowd.

Eadie had not seen her own father for a long time and she had almost forgotten what he looked like. She knew for sure that this was a daddy-type, and she wondered why she found him so peculiarly offensive.

He soothed the anguish of the teacher, who was relieved that she had not had to face the legendary Siddy Church. She watched Reggie; he doesn't blink, thought Eadie on the ride home.

It was a mystery to Eadie why her mother had clung so desperately to the professed undying love for Frankie Wilt. Now she was easily giving it up to chase this Reggie. In a household like Siddy Church's, a course that ran counter to the feelings of the house was a fatal drawback. Paddy's resolution to love this man was received with dismay.

A topic returned to each day was the crude human nature of Paddy's projected new beau. This red-haired Reggie Spicer. He was assiduously cocksure and, with that absurd moustache, incapable of finding a fellow traveller in this house of aunties. Into their ranks, he would never be accepted. His manly courage was still worth something, even though they all treated him like a goblin. He tried to weave a sort of Wild West domination over the women. Initially, Eadie Wilt had wanted to like him. She climbed on his knee and had been reassured with lollies. She chewed till her gums ached. She felt her mouth being ravaged by the constant crunching of boiled humbugs and sticky, jaw-breaking toffees.

"Your mum's a wild machine, Eadie Wilt," he told

her, and Eadie felt like she was going to be sick. He always grabbed Eadie and rubbed his moustache into her neck. Since paternity was not a guiding theme in this house, the women took this vaudevillian fathering very badly. Everyone had to be very careful because Paddy's mysterious sentimental self had been asserting itself. The awful man was clouded in a misty romantic persona.

"Will you be staying much longer?" the aunties asked him with their eyes. Eadie squirmed away from him after a while, and she developed an aversion for cheap sweets that stayed with her for the rest of her life. She did not like the way he rubbed her knees. His palms felt wet and furry. She did not like the way his teeth flashed or the smell of his mouth when he came close. If she did not like all of this, then she hated going on drives with him and Paddy on Sunday afternoons.

All in all, Paddy was a little brighter when Reggie was around, but everyone hated him. After a while he vanished and Paddy's sentimental self took a rest. Willy Howe, who met Eadie during the flood, told her that Reggie Spicer owed the bookie a lot of money.

After he left, Grandma Siddy said to Eadie, "If you don't get everything you want, think of the things you don't get that you don't want."

Eadie knew exactly what she did not want: a daddy-type like Reggie Spicer. She was happy that she would not have to go on Sunday drives any more. She liked to go out with Willy Howe in her rickety bus with carburettor problems. They would look for bush tucker. They came home with a basket of dried-up morsels and sometimes some lush mushrooms. Willy Howe was vigorous, and she knew the disarmingly beautiful ravines and rivers where they could dangle their legs in the water and Willy could leap and catch a fish with her bare hands.

"We're having fun today." She would smile her toothless smile and Eadie would lean near and smell her burning-green-wood smell full of secrets.

When Eadie's father made his one-time visit, Willy Howe was not there. She would have liked him, thought Eadie, for his magic. It was in the flood that Eadie came across Willy Howe. Willy drove a ute. Willy had schooled Eadie in wondrous and terrifying things. She wanted lots of grog, then. Now Willy Howe had all her children taken away from her. Even the seventh one had died at birth after the flood. She didn't seem to like the grog much any more.

"Too much terrifying things," she told Eadie, but her laughter dispelled the morbid promise.

During the flood, she had slept with Willy Howe in the back of the ute under the tarp. Willy's children all roamed about or hung around the shearers' shed where a big fire was kept burning and smoking while it rained and rained for weeks on end. Sometimes men came to get Willy Howe and Eadie would hide under the tarp. Men from the town, ones that Eadie knew from the pub, came and made Willy take out their dicks and suck until they pushed her off in the mud. Eadie saw it and she watched the men's faces with the rain coming down on their heads and their eyes closed.

"All the men like that," she told Eadie Wilt. Eadie could not imagine her grandmother sucking a dick.

"Oh yes," Willy told her, "she probably has, your grandmother. In the old days, your men came to our old place and took all the young girls and chained them to trees out in the scrub."

"They're not 'our' men," said Eadie. "We don't have any men, just Joe Flood." She did not like the tone of this story but Willy Howe was making a fire for them and it suddenly came alive and Willy wrapped her strong bony arms around the child. They had found an old house, and the fire and warmth were good. The story diminished into incoherent mutterings, and they sat there with their feet and legs almost in the fire. Eadie had been wet for so long that she cried as she felt the dry heat in her arms and her hair fluffing out from her head in a dry fuzz. As they were falling asleep, she asked, "Why did they chain the women to the trees?"

Willy Howe let out a grotesque sigh of tiredness. She was bone sober and she didn't rattle on when she hadn't had a drink.

"Well! Them men, they were all sore with sickness of their dicks and they believed that if they been coming to our girls that those girls would take on that sickness and it would go from them men."

The originality of this idea was full of light and dark feeling when told by Willy Howe. Eadie fell immediately asleep, not being able to think it all out. She was too little after all. Her eyes were big and she looked up at Willy's face in the firelight and suddenly she was very tired.

When Willy Howe came to live at the big old hotel, they tried to keep Eadie Wilt away from her. Then, for a while, they decided that Willy and Eadie were an excellent combination. When they were together, no trouble occurred. They kept each other busy. Especially after Joe Flood died and Mantel Bonlevi had been killed. Everyone was lapsing into heartbreak and no one could give Eadie Wilt much time any more.

Of course, Willy Howe went bush a lot, coming and going as she pleased. She was not there when Reggie Spicer was coming into her mother's bed with all his muddle and confusion. Once, he was there in the morning when Eadie woke up and she saw her mother all small and dark against his white fleshy leg. Long coils of dark hair fell across his cock. Eadie felt a surging swirling scream come into her throat. Paddy jumped up and whacked her and pulled her from the room by her hair. She pulled her pale green Chinese dressing gown on and pulled Eadie down the passage. All the aunties came out in their under-clothes and snatched her away and into one of their rooms. There were white marks on the sunny skin, and her ears were ringing. The morning was hushed.

Had Eadie been more precocious, no doubt she would have complained about the fondlings of Reggie Spicer. The aunties, anticipating something of this sort, began taking Eadie into the linen cupboard and asking all sorts of questions about Reggie.

It all stopped when the man disappeared, and Eadie settled into reading the new books that Grandma Siddy had given her for her birthday. Eadie noticed that Paddy's tempestuous moments were rare now. She was often dead-tired from working in the kitchen over the wood stove. Sometimes Eadie would watch her from the dark corners where her bed was in the deep recess. Her mother would come into the room from her bath, her beautiful dark face scrubbed and shiny with the towel, turban-like, holding her dark, wet hair. She smoothed her bed and took out the drawers from her dressing table and began folding things. Eadie could see she looked very peaceful. It was fascinating, Eadie could barely believe it. She wanted to run over and climb into her mother's lap and ask her, Are we happy now? She knew better than that. If she got out of bed now she might get a smack, and once Paddy gave one smack you could not stop her. Sometimes when she had been drinking, she would come into the room, turn on all the lights, fling back the covers on Eadie and pull her from the bed by her hair. Sometimes Eadie wet the bed in fright. Sometimes the anger would subside and Paddy would collapse into a suffocating heap beside her daughter. They would fall into each other and rock back and forward as if they had both been attacked by some outside force. Sometimes Eadie helped Paddy into bed and then she would hop back into her bed smelling of her own urine. She slept in the wet bed and crept down to the linen closet next morning for clean sheets. The aunties had given her a plastic sheet to put under the linen so she wouldn't get into more trouble.

Much later, when Paddy was dying and Eadie sat with her for the first times in her life and talked about the old days, Paddy told her how she admired her for not doing all that stuff to her own children. Later, when her mother went into the hospital and she waited for the final profound message, Paddy opened her eyes and smiled that sweet dark smile and said, "Don't wait around here, go home and clean out the fridges, luv."

That night when Eadie returned to the hospital at visiting hours, Paddy was gone. The room was clean, the bed empty, newly made, tight as a drum. Eadie was desperate. "Where's my mum?" she cried to the nurses at their station. No one had rung her. Eadie cried, "Where's my mum?" but they shushed her and said, No, she could not see her, it was not the policy of the hospital. Eadie could not understand why she cried so much at Paddy's funeral. Something awful had trespassed on her heart, gripped it vice-like and squeezed it with surprising strength.

Moving on with the Wordstretcher

Eadie said she had seen all manner of dying. Ethereal, delicate and humorous dying. Some of the aunties died in the big hotel. She held the fragile old hands and whispered something celestial. It was a time, she thought, to conjure up beautiful words. Well-built words for lost confidence. She would speak of something golden, even as she watched the bile seeping from the old mouth. Eadie, the wordstretcher, would squeeze the old hand and develop her tale. Her enthusiasm, the nerve of her descriptions of the after-life, gave consolation, and many an auntie died laughing.

Sometimes she stumbled over some rare hitherto unrevealed notion, some oceanic rage, a deluge of torture and exorcism. She laid her head down on the heart, one debonair auntie had an attack of hiccups and with a good whiff of laughter, joined the holy bosses with the most voluptuous death belch. A thousand, stuttering, crackling, tropical sounds electrically charged the room. A prestigious aristocratic death, thought Siddy Church. Death was considered by the aunties to be the poisonous artery of life but Eadie had flown with their restless spirits out past the great desert plateau of her imagination, in a hundred thousand fragments, flying, flying.

Of course, Paddy said, "Get her out of here," if she was found at the deathbed. Eadie was sought after and asked for by the dying. Paddy wondered if her feet were cloven. Eadie could sit by a bed, stopped in time. She did not notice the slight stench in the room and she listened to everything. The mad desires, she found them instructive. Sometimes they talked dirty to the little girl and then died belly up in a mystical frenzy. She rubbed their twisted hands; old moths precariously balanced on the great wall between worlds.

Eadie did not jump to any wild conclusions about death, its paradises or its purgatories. Even though the aunties were succumbing to its ecclesiastic authority. The big fat trap of God had not overwhelmed her, not when she saw the room fill with wickedly erotic sylphs flying around the room like confetti.

Siddy Church said, "I'm fed up with dying. I'm selling up and moving on." She swept away the ambiguities of life's tendency to botch up promises and shocked the whole town by announcing that she would marry again. Surrounded by aunties, she did just that.

He was much younger, and the town's whisper was that he had driven into town in a truck and driven out in a Chrysler. That the Chrysler was battered and worn out did not spoil the feeling of the story. The general notion was that an opportunist truck driver had taken advantage of the beloved Siddy Church. This was the last story they told in that town about Siddy Church before she moved on.

The whole town gathered on the great lawn the day they left. Siddy kissed the wall that Mantel had been trapped behind. A semi-trailer was loaded up with their belongings. The long train of Holden utes and Morris Minors, with the Chrysler at the rear, headed out of town in the direction of Melbourne.

"Yes," said Siddy Church, "we are going to live the city life." Willy Howe and her dog stood in the road until she could see them no more.

They sang songs on the way, swapped cars, drank tea on the roadside and picked up hitchhikers who were shoved in the back with someone's tea chest. A lot of laughing and crying was done on this journey. Halfway there, they stopped at a friend's. They stayed on this farm for a time.

Eadie bathed with the farmer's children in an old tub in the paddock. The bath was filled with water from the tank and topped up with Lux flakes. Eadie loved it. The cows stood about. It was very frothy. That was all she could remember.

Eadie Wilt took to city life. She liked it as much as the country. She was supposed to go to her room after school since Paddy thought there were more dangers in the city. Her mother worked the bar until six o'clock closing. A warmed-up counter-lunch was brought up to Eadie by an auntie. Eadie Wilt's room looked like this: two windows that faced on to a tram-track and a very busy inner-city street. Across the road was the Queen Victoria Market. Four days a week, there were traffic jams and fruiterers bringing in their produce from the growers. Eadie liked the bustle of market days. She especially liked Greeks and Italians. Sometimes she would get up at four o'clock in the morning and ride between the market stalls in a trolley, listening to the music of the place.

The workers' union had breakfast meetings at Siddy Church's place. Some of the men carried guns, and heated arguments got Siddy moving towards her big black bag. One autumn, a dispute caused a gun battle to occur between the stalls in full view of shoppers. The coppers came around all the time asking questions and wanting free drinks. Siddy said it was like the old days when Joe Flood brought home his commie mates.

Eadie Wilt was seeing how the other half lived too. She went into houses where fathers belted their kids in front of her, and once she saw her friend's mother thrown down the stairs. She told her friend that she would get her grandma's gun, and they didn't let Eadie in their house again.

Siddy Church's hair had gone completely, gloriously white. It was a fine head of hair. She was still strong enough to throw out an offensive drunk. Eadie often saw her at the bar quietly reprimanding a cowering man about his vagrant fists. The offended woman would be upstairs with her cut eye and broken arm, hiding out. If the man did not see reason, then she would send Paulie to double-up on the warning.

"Learn the lesson quick," she would tell the husband. Siddy had her own private way. If it worked or not, they never knew. Years later when Eadie thought she was intelligent, she would go to Siddy with her troubles.

"We'll send Paulie over," Siddy told her.

Paulie by this time was seventy-five. His fists had fossilised into balls of mutton raised in the air up near his strangely childlike ears.

Siddy's new husband grew to love her like his mother. She dressed him well, and he drove smart silly cars. Once when Siddy had a gallstone operation, he thought she was dying and panicked. He sold her string of pearls and ran away with a young widow from the Lions' Club. Siddy recovered and he came back. He was pleased to have his "mumma" back. Thirty or so years later, she did really die. He had been mostly in his bed for the two or three years prior to this. They had bought a house in a leafy suburb with big back yards. Siddy was happy. She grew vegetables and had an elaborate chook house. She had great-grandchildren because Eadie Wilt had her own children by then. Siddy Church spoilt her boy. She made him special desserts and he wasted all their money on the T.A.B. She had stopped him from driving because he crashed into fences and weaved hopelessly in and out of traffic like Mr McGoo.

Without warning, Siddy went down. They took her to hospital where she lay with strange gaping ulcers appearing on her legs.

"They are my sins," she told Eadie.

She had wild dreams about the ward being shot up and people coming through walls that could open and close and concertina like a squeeze-box. She hallucinated enjoyably for weeks and kept everybody entertained.

When she came home, she was almost bedridden. Two old aunties were there and the youngish husband. He was twenty years Siddy's junior and could still find his way in the kitchen. Eadie Wilt made her best vegetable soup, thick with barley, and visited her grandmother.

Siddy sat in the front bedroom in her bedjacket. The winter sun streamed softly into the freezing house.

"I'm not cold," said Siddy. "I don't feel the cold."

It was true, thought Eadie, feeling a lump of inexplicable regret in her throat. Her grandmother went all winter with bare legs and arms.

"Working women don't feel the cold," Siddy mumbled. Her eyes were watery, and they held Eadie; when they hugged, the elder woman would not let go.

She pulled back the covers of her bed. All around her bandaged legs, there were objects: old pink gold brooches and strands of pearls and solid brassy vases and rolls of money tied up with handkerchiefs. Siddy Church did not trust banks. All her life, no matter where her grand-daughter travelled or what lifestyle she had adopted, Siddy would send her two pounds every week. Later, when currency changed, two dollars. Eadie lost on that one. On Fridays, Siddy went to the post office with a letter, which for twenty-five years had said exactly the same thing, word for word. She would add the two-dollar note and lick the envelope shut. Sometimes Eadie was in a country with poor postal services and she would get a six-month supply all at once. Eadie wanted to wallpaper her room with these identical letters and envelopes. She said they told her life's story. She said that if she had been Andy Warhol she would have done it.

Siddy opened her mouth for the spoonful of soup. Norman, the younger husband, had already finished his. Eadie knew that they were being fed by her aunt in the evening. She wondered why they were both so ravenous, so greedily anxious in their eating.

Eadie climbed into bed with her grandmother. Waves of memory enveloped them. Mists of secret thought, strange and hidden, passed between the two. Caught in the tangle, silent vivid declarations. They looked into each other's eyes and felt the pulse of promise. Believing absolutely in the supernatural, Eadie saw clearly the beautiful white robes of angels persist at Siddy's shoulders. Around the soft down of her neck, they settled. When the soup was finished and several hours had gone by, Siddy Church told

Eadie, "When I'm gone, go and ask Aunt for half."

This was her inheritance. Eadie smiled to herself. The eyes were closed. Eadie put her head down to the lustrous white head; her childhood sanctuary, its billowing waves no longer held in place by the customary hairnet. The mouth was still impudent, turned up at the corners, ready to smile out. She seemed to be sleeping. Eadie readied herself to go, but the grip on her hand was too strong.

"Don't leave me, Eadie."

Eadie thought she heard that, but the lips were still. She knew that Siddy Church would never leave her.

She sat with the sleeping woman who had given her the mysterious rudimentary rites that she was now struggling to throw off.

Her old room at the pub, opposite the market, was stacked high with Siddy Church's stuff. There were refrigerators and washing machines and fur coats and boxes of cigars off the back of a truck, and so much else.

Eadie Wilt could often be seen by the market people, hanging out of the window over the tram-tracks. A child smoking a cigarette in dodgy make-up in a beguiling hat. "In her own world," they said of her and laughed. It was anyone's guess, where that was. When she got bored with being in her room, she climbed out of the upstairs gents' toilet window, down the plumbing pipes, into the lanes and passageways of other people's houses. Once, she left the bathroom window open and thieves got into the hotel and stole things. No one could work out how they got in because she climbed in this window and locked it before the theft was discovered.

Now she was beginning to be a bold cheeky girl. More and more, she escaped from the hotel and roamed the streets. Sometimes she didn't go to school either. She liked being bad, the mystery of it.

At the time when Eadie looked like becoming a delinquent, Siddy promised to buy her a piano. In her room, Eadie daydreamed about the piano, imagined it there beside the window. She looked down at the people on market days. They waved at her. She knew that when she played this piano, the music would swell out from her window and stop traffic. Her grandmother, however, was very slow in keeping the promise. In fact, she seemed to have forgotten the undertaking altogether.

It was the first time in all her life that Eadie questioned her grandmother. She watched her closely for other flaws - listening to her meandering stories with a critical ear. She often told people across the bar that she was intending to purchase a new piano.

"It's for Eadie," she'd tell with a honeyed tone, and everyone drank to it with witless smiles of appreciation for Siddy's grandmotherly generosity.

However, no piano arrived. Eadie had been good for so long that a roar in her chest told her that she could not do it for much longer. Her enthusiasm for her grandmother was sinking, along with a mystic longing for the promised piano.

It was Paddy who finally brought the matter to a head. She told her mother to buy the piano or belt up. She said it in her dark refined way in front of the entire saloon bar. That did it. Siddy's hands went deep into her apron pockets, and with several aunties, Paddy and Eadie, they all trudged up the hill of Victoria Street to peer in the windows of Lamberti Brothers.

There were many advisors; all the talk was of pianos and piano players. It was Saturday morning. The spectacle of the piano coming down the steep hill in Victoria Street on coasters, with the aunties trying to stop it accelerating and killing pedestrians, was not soon forgotten.

Eadie could not adjust her heartbeats. It seemed too big an episode ever to forget. Her excitement throbbed, the crowd parted and yelled wildly as the mob plunged down the road, amidst the traffic, with the stampeding piano. Bystanders applauded as they finally brought the thing to a standstill outside the pub. It came easily through the double doors of the saloon bar but the internal doors, the ones that led to the staircase to Eadie's room, were too narrow. Eadie's heart thrashed around with some hostility as the drinkers put their grog on the polished surface of the lid. They did make way for a ceremonious introduction of the child to her new piano. Then they got on with the matter of everyone having a go and playing every groggy shanty that had ever been sung.

Still, Eadie did not give up. She came downstairs

early in the morning, before even Siddy was up, to play the piano. She taught herself songs and sang along gleefully in the early hours of the morning. It was still dark outside and, in the saloon bar, there was no one to hear her orchestral inventions. She would polish the piano with Marveer and an old singlet before she went to school.

In the afternoons, there would be beer splashings all over her polishings. Occasionally, someone would come in who could play well, a groggy Debussy perhaps, or some Cole Porter. Finally, Eadie went back to being bad and forgot about the piano. It stayed in the saloon bar until Siddy retired and brought it to the house where she would die. It was in the spare room on the last day that Eadie saw her grandmother. She ran her fingers over its scars. Siddy kept it polished and always referred to it as Eadie's piano. Eadie upset Norman that day by sitting at the piano and playing an exhilarating tune. She trilled and bellowed vulgarly. Norman thought privately that it was probably this that killed Siddy Church.

Eadie kept humming and went back to Siddy's bedside. She saw the big black handbag sticking out from under the covers. Siddy cradled it to her. Inside was the pearl-handled derringer pistol that she always kept close by. Eadie moved all the stuff aside and took the great soft woman in her arms. She held her tightly and gave it her best shot. This last embracing hug will have to last a long time, she thought. Norman had gone back to his bench in the garden.

Eadie hummed and rocked her grandmother and whispered all the splendid and wondrous words that she had ever heard. She saw that her grandma wore "rags". They hung down between those sweet old legs, held up by two giant safety pins. She wondered if her insides were bleeding out of her. She rocked her from side to side. It was warm, it felt good. Eadie Wilt was nearly forty years of age but her childhood continued with emphatic certainty until that day when Siddy Church gave it all up with easy acceptance.

Norman arranged the funeral. He took Eadie by the arm. "Come and look at gran, she looks beautiful." She was dressed in a coloured dress with a cheap sheen and Eadie roared aloud that Siddy did not wear colour or shine. He cheeks were rouged and a purple waxy lipstick had been applied badly. Eadie gasped in shock, pushed back the satin in fury. The old legs were encased in nylons and the feet forced into shoes that Siddy would not have been seen dead in. Eadie said this aloud and many of the aunties enjoyed the pun. No one moved to stop her as she set the feet free and threw the pumps in amongst the wreaths behind the fake fountain. Nor did anyone tut or sigh when she wet her hankie and rubbed off the rouge and the purple lipstick. It set the stage for a perfect funeral. Everyone relaxed and spoke loudly and a great deal of laughter and tears were enjoyed. Siddy lay amongst them, what was left of her. Her impudent mouth was kissed by just about everybody.

Eadie Wilt Meets Anna Wesoloski

Eadie Wilt knew Anna Wesoloski for the briefest time. If Eadie thought of one word for Anna, it was ancient. The truth was that Anna had been a girl so similar to Eadie that Anna fancied that they were of the same girl print, one that repeated itself in many corners of this wild world. Her seeing was so the same that when Anna first met Eadie, she thought secretly, "There I am." Eadie was not to know this, of course, because all she could see was ancient. A very lean, whipped out, old body and a face so marked by age that Eadie thought Anna must have lived for one hundred years.

Their first conversation was horses. Where Eadie came from, everyone knew horses. Eadie said her family could ride like the wind.

"Sometimes wind is very erratic," responded Anna Wesoloski to this piece of information. To Eadie, horses were not part of fantasy tales of young girls with a horse of their own, but rather part of rural life. Siddy Church had always owned horses, until they came to live in the city. To see Siddy riding was a fine sight. A bushwoman of considerable skill, she had often ridden with Mantel and the aunties to the

Lake District. Eadie had gone with them. Even Paddy was truly pleasant in the saddle. She smiled more than usual, and the aunties sighed when they saw her on a horse.

Anna exhausted the subject of horses in their first conversation but Eadie saw the agile smile, the quickness in the girl behind the ancient. The lines disappeared, Anna's voice young and nubile as she sat astride imaginary mares, mounted the dappled stallions of her youth. She said she had been taught to sew. She said that had saved her from an early death.

Anna Wesoloski was not listened to in her own home. Her daughter Gertrude and her grandson Gerald switched off and didn't hear a thing.

She was old, much older than anyone Eadie had seen or heard. Much older than Siddy Church or old great-grandmother on the Wilt side. Anna knew there was not much time and she still had a great deal to tell. She never left the house, and hardly anyone came to visit. Until this Eadie Wilt. She came just in time, towards the very last. She listened steadfastly and even wrote things down when she went back to her own house down the street.

Eventually, Eadie would know the rest of this family very well and Anna would be overshadowed in the lovestakes. From time to time, however, Eadie would stumble over a memory and be surprised how bright and clear Anna remained.

Later in life, people asked Eadie why she had Anna

Wesoloski embroidered on her sheets. She would explain simply, "They belonged to her and now they belong to me."

Anna came from another continent. She had lived in many countries, she said, ones that you would never find on a map. They were in another hemisphere and no one acted as you could ever expect. She said she had even met murderers. Men who massacred whole towns. She could talk about them calmly, their manners and the other side of them. She talked of all these things with this girl.

Anna Wesoloski could sit at her front window and see down the whole length of the street. She was always excited when she saw the young girl coming. She'd knock over things in her haste to catch Eadie as she passed the letterbox. As soon as she could catch her breath, she started in telling it all. Strange metaphors poured out. Anna spoke a faulty English and Eadie one of her own making but they understood each other perfectly.

"She truly speaks," Anna told her grandson. "You should marry her when she grows up."

Their conversations followed no order. They both instinctively knew that no story could ever be told chronologically. Each day had its moments that reached back to other days in the past and stretched forward to days not yet lived.

Eadie thought that Anna made things a whole lot more interesting in this leafy street, and she was dazzled by her mimicry. Eadie told Anna that her mother had just married a nice bloke and that they had moved to the suburbs to begin a new life.

"Mmm," said Anna, "I came here to end a very old one." Eadie was glad to meet Anna. She almost stopped missing life in the pub. It seemed you could pick up aunties anywhere.

Truly Speak

Eadie Wilt stood in her singlet and cottontails, nibbling canapés. She felt like Aphrodite. Her centres were balanced; winter closed around. She had no festering resentments. She was in love transit. A sweet green garden summoned her to the window. This was "truly speak". She did feel good.

She had written a first draft for a story about the street that she had moved to after those childhood years in old hotels. The wonder of living in a real house. It was unexpected. No one thought that Paddy would fall in love with a decent bloke like Hardy. Paddy was all burnt out from cooking over the wood stove and mashing spuds. She still pined after the husband that she'd walked out on. A lot of passion and fury kept the wild machine running amok, but the random terrorism was mysteriously familiar and it did not scare Eadie so much anymore. When Hardy came along, he embraced Paddy with conversation. He liked birdcalls and new landscapes. His life was not one that created a stir. A half-peace settled on Paddy and she prepared herself to be loved forever. They moved away from Siddy Church and the aunties. A blue marriage ceremony took place. They found a house and turned it into a guesthouse. The bungalows in the backyard were perfect for this. Eadie Wilt had her first kiss while living in this house. It happened the night she went to the town hall to get her inoculation.

"Tonight you should walk down there and have your injection," her mother told her.

Eadie was already in her pyjamas and dressing-gown and didn't want to go.

"Just go like that. It's a warm night. Hurry up! You'll miss out."

No one argued with Paddy when she started to get worked up, and she showed every sign of it right now. It was dark. There were only two street-lights between her house and the town hall. When Eadie entered the hall, it was ludicrously bright and hot and when she looked around she saw that no one else was dressed in their pyjamas. She felt stupid, her face flushed red. On top of that, she hated injections. She got in line after they gave her a card, and after fifteen minutes she was pricked and was able to make her way through the gossiping crowd to go home. Behind her in the queue was a smirking man with a sports coat cast with sardonic negligence about his shoulders. He looked right in her face while she was being injected and grinned as she winced and swallowed hard. She did feel a festering resentment then; her centres were not balanced. She gave out an utterance of hurt when the needle went in, and pulled the face of victim which she knew no one found attractive.

She got out quick. As she relaxed into the warm night, the prickly heat feeling left her. She rubbed her arm. Cars went by and people talked in groups walking behind her. When she turned into her street, it became silent except for a soft footstep nearby. She listened to hear if it was a man or woman. She could not tell. A wild guess: it's a woman, and she turned to look. It was the smirking man with the sports coat. She was almost twelve. He was dangerously twenty. She had still a small smile at the guessing game and kept it because she had reached her gate and turned in to home turf. A spring came into her step and she almost skipped down the side yard. The light was on in her mother's bedroom. Paddy would be reading in bed. She was startled to hear the footsteps still behind her at the back door. She pushed open the wire door and he caught it and stopped it from banging. He brought his face immediately up to hers without bringing his body or hands anywhere near her. She felt her lips being sucked towards him. He was holding her mouth in a suction of teeth and lips and tongue. She had a panic attack. Didn't he know about Paddy, her mother? After a minute, he let her lips go and gave her a good look at him. His face was impeccable. Luscious black hair and deep pool eyes. A wonderous gem of a brow. His crooked mouth was submitting prettily to the do-badder pout. Then he was gone because all the lights were being turned on and Paddy was asking her what took so long.

Long after the wondrous heyday of childhood had

passed, Eadie remembered the boy with the aromatic mouth who drifted to her through the wide flowerbeds of summer. The rasp of cicadas filled the night and those few seconds of human contact could be revived after years of neglect. Though she experienced a trill, a warming of the earth, she did not consider this a sexual encounter. If the boy grew into a mature and serious stalker of young girls, she never knew.

Later when women were talking freely of fear and genitals or orgasms, this old memory was dished out, and murmured amongst them was the belief that this was Eadie Wilt's first orgasm. The scattering of kept moments, to be brought together with all the others, was Eadie's problem. Each moment always reminded her of another. She moved constantly through the revolving doors of deja vu. This boy was like the one who had roamed the passages at the pub, she told herself. He had knocked on her door. No one knocked on her door. This was her private place. No one may knock. Grandma Siddy came to store her goods that she had fenced, and Eadie received these like great and wondrous gifts. Even she did not knock. Siddy would signal and Eadie would open her door and receive the goods excitedly. Now this man knocked in passing on the way to his room. He was a truck driver, young and brash, from Bundoora. He had greasy black hair that hung untidily forward, and he had seen Eadie hanging out of her second-floor window when he was parking his truck. This greasy man-boy stayed at the pub on his nights in town.

When Eadie hung out of the window with her black hair cut in the Chinese style, everyone laughed and she waved to all the people she knew, and others that she didn't. So the boy knocked. That was his game, and Eadie didn't answer. That was hers. Sometimes he knocked for a long time and said things like, "I know you're in there. Let me in." She would creep around inside until he passed by.

The only thing that changed in the game was that one night he was blind drunk, and knocked and banged on the door. Eadie opened the door and he fell right in. He had been crying in his beer and Siddy Church had kicked him out of the bar. Now he lay elegantly, half in the dark passage and half in Eadie's room. The child fought a desperate battle with his flaying limbs to get him out of the room. Paddy would be coming up soon. "What is going on?" she would say and she would not be easily convinced that nothing was. Eadie was feeling desperate. She thought of going downstairs and getting her grandmother. She started to drag him out of the room by his feet, but he was suddenly startlingly alive. He kicked her hand away and crawled on all fours into her room and climbed into a teabox standing on its side against the wall. Just then, the shadow of Paddy loomed on the stair and Eadie could hear her conversation with one of the aunties twisting down the winding passage. Eadie did a flamboyant jump into her room and closed the door. She turned the radio on and threw a blanket over the teabox and a pile of her dress-ups over the legs sticking out. The man stayed still, except for the odd snort. Paddy felt comforted by the radio noise.

Ignoring the invasion of her inner world, Eadie plugged away at her homework, secure in the knowledge that no one would knock at her door any more that night. She knew that the delinquent in the box, upon whom she would now have to exert an influence, would become undrunk after a while. One ear was on him, his snorting and snoring. The room was semi-arid with his smell.

No great harm was done by the man in the teabox, though he slept there all night. Dawn offered a mirror-bright sky and an offence-free escape. He shrank, as he gathered his self together. He heard muffled gnomic utterances coming from the other side of the room. Hidden by a massive pile of junk was Eadie Wilt on her small bed. She was looking at her image in the mirror. From his backstage vantage, he accommodated himself to the role-playing of the child. Balancing a generous portion of wonderment with an uncomfortable feeling of danger, he yanked on his jeans that somehow managed to be around his ankles. He immediately thought of the full-blown woman in the bar. Her cobalt eyes flashed like pilot lights and he knew this was no occasion to relax. Something banged between his ears. He remembered talking to the child and trying to take off his pants between sentences. He had fleshed her out to be a woman in his mind. The child heard his melodramas and came around the furniture piles to shush him. He gasped as he saw her restless infant face. She did not conform to his imagination at all. She knelt and whispered rational directions, tidying up his ideas. The tension drained from him as she helped him from the box to the door. As he made the long voyage down the passage, he passed Siddy Church on her way to light "the donkey". This was the hot water service. It was coal-fuel, and lit at five-thirty every morning, before Siddy took her shot of whisky. She put her guiding hand on his shoulder and her refined, demanding eye questioned him.

That day, Eadie Wilt forgot all about him. She had Betty Wright, her new best friend at school, to think about. Later, in the convoluted form of memory, she simply gathered these men together, the backdoor kissing boy and the man in the teabox who never returned to the hotel and everyone wondered why.

The other starkly beautiful boy was remembered for forty summers, especially when the thin lace of dew was lifting from the garden beneath her window. Then she would lift a hand in greeting to him. She daren't give herself airs, more than this.

A photo essay from that time shows Eadie still a child exploring the vanities and set agendas of approaching womanhood. People talked about Eadie's growth as if it would never happen. It seemed important. She climbed on the garage roof and let the willow tree hang itself over her. She let herself grow. "I'm growing," she said, looking down her short little body.

Mr Mott and the Bathing Beauty

Caulfield was the suburb that Paddy and Hardy had chosen for their new beginning. Eadie Wilt supposed that it was short for cauliflower fields. She closed her eyes on the way there and imagined rows of cauliflowers.

Eadie Wilt roamed around by herself. She wagged school and walked underground along the drains that ran under several suburbs and came out at St Kilda Beach. She would swim out from the beach to a moored boat and spend the day lying on the deck pretending to be at sea. In the late afternoon she would return home, her cheeks sunburnt, her nose and shoulders peeling, her shoes full of sand. Paddy always looked suspicious. A bitter struggle continued between them. Something bad was happening to Eadie. She was looking miserable.

It was all on account of the boarder, the one in the third bungalow. Paddy was happy that the four bungalows in the backyard all had a tenant at last. The four men sat at the dining table every night with Hardy and Eadie, while Paddy served them fatty meats with boiled carrots.

"What's the matter with you, Eadie?" asked Paddy.

"It's Mr Mott," said Eadie wishing that her grand-mother Siddy still lived with them. "Shhh!" said Paddy. "He's following me," sniffled Eadie. "What *are* you talking about?" said Paddy outraged. She sent Eadie flying with a shove, across the room.

It was no joke. Everywhere she went, the lispy-voiced boarder followed. At night he would creep around the side of the house and stand at her window. It had a wire screen but the window was open and the light from inside was bright. The teachers wrote to Paddy that something was wrong with Eadie. This expanding whodunit did not persuade Paddy that something was really wrong. Paddy knew intuitively that *everything* was always wrong.

On Friday nights, Paddy and Hardy went out. Eadie, at the beginning of the marriage, had been taken on these excursions but now they left her home by herself.

"It's all right," reasoned Paddy. "In an emergency, the boarders are there."

"But I don't like him. He looks in the window."

She pointed to the venetian blinds that Paddy had just finished cleaning. Paddy brought her vibrant face down to the child's level to demonstrate her sincerity.

"Everyone thinks that there is someone looking in the window when they're home alone, *but there never is!*"

Eadie wondered how someone as stupid as Paddy could be born to a mother as wise as Siddy Church.

That night, however, when she was sitting in the

living room by herself, she felt someone at the window. She repeated what her mother said; there is never anyone there. It worked. She felt a long-awaited safeness expand her night. She meddled with her mother's things, especially the ones that she was forbidden to touch. An hour went by before she grew tired of the game. She turned off the lamps and prepared to cross the hall to her own room. Her eyes went to the venetian blinds, still half-open. She went closer despite what her mother had said. He *was* there! Inches away, looking in; and he smiled. She did not know why, but she felt a crushing in her chest and her legs dragged her down. A car's headlights came up the drive. Eadie could hear Mr Mott greet Paddy. Eadie went quickly to her own room and hopped into bed fully dressed.

Paddy was seriously drunk, pissed to the eyeballs. Her new beginning was in disarray. She thought in her confused state that she might never make a life without Siddy. She drank three times as much as Hardy. With formidable tact he had dragged her from the party.

As they turned into the driveway, Mr Mott walked into the headlights smiling. He came to the window on Paddy's side. He looked her over with superior curious eyes. Paddy lurched inside. She went straight to Eadie's room and snapped on the light. If the child had been asleep, all this rattle and bang would have woken her. She was scared. Paddy stood over her and peered down. Something looked wrong. She pulled back the covers. Eadie was fully dressed. What so infuriated her about a child in bed with her clothes on? Eadie never knew. She gave a fierce cry, grabbed, with two fists, her girl's hair and lifted her in a great savage haul that ripped the baby skull and bloodied her own nails. The child hit the dresser on the other side of the room. A scream pierced the night and Paddy kicked and punched at the bundle at her feet. Tears flooded her face, her mouth stretched in anger. Then she was gone, and all was still except for the small creepy whine that Eadie knew was herself. Eadie's spirit resigned itself to a hideous fate.

Paddy was up early next day. She hardly looked at Eadie. Eadie left for school. She walked down the street and caught the tram. She felt like that rare phenomenon that Siddy Church always talked about: "an old soul". When she came to the school gate, she detoured and headed for the stormwater drain.

It took her an hour or more to walk to the beach. When she came out into daylight, the beach was deserted. No one knew where she was, and she felt sheltered. She walked along the pier and sat on the wooden steps that led to the water. She curled on the ledge and slept. She needed this sleep. With sleep, all was mended. The sun was out and there was water all about. When Eadie woke, it was a different, radiant world. Two women fished from the jetty near the kiosk. She climbed down to the rocks and took off her school dress with its green checkered pattern. She was in her undies and singlet, but they were navy-blue and looked like a swimsuit. From the rocks, she could watch the people on the sand. People stopped and talked to her. She walked down to Little Jerusalem, so-called, because all the Jewish people sat there. On Tuesday, the sea baths closed its doors to the public so the nuns from Loreto Convent could swim. Eadie would swim down to the back, amongst the jellyfish, where the rusty bars separated the pool from the ocean. The nuns came early, before the crowds came out, and Eadie could see them with their habits off. This was Eadie's favourite thing to do, until the day that she met the bathing beauty.

The bathing beauty appeared on the sand one day and took everyone's breath away. She was like no other beauty Eadie had ever seen. She did not have long legs or big tits or blue eyes. She was short and stocky and her hair had a million tight curls that went everywhere and tumbled down her back as well. She was cocoa-coloured. Everything that she turned up was shell pink, her palms, and the soles of her pretty feet. She spoke to Eadie, and they walked along the beachfront together from the pier to Little Jerusalem. Here they sat on the wall. The bathing beauty wore a bikini, and Eadie wore her navy-blue briefs and singlet. No one wore bikinis in Melbourne in those days, so a crowd gathered and a newspaper-man took their photographs. The bathing beauty was Eadie Wilt's new best friend.

Eadie tried to stay out of her mother's way. On Saturday, Paddy told her to stay home while she and

Hardy went to the market. Everyone seemed to be out, so Eadie read under a tree. Out of nowhere came the smashing of glass and branches breaking and the sounds of someone making "ah . . . ah . . ." sounds. Eadie was on her feet and traced the site of the calamity. It was Mr Mott. He had fallen through the skylight on the garage roof. He lay on the concrete floor of the garage. The two doors were wide open and he looked like a culprit, "up to something bad", thought Eadie.

Now, she never turned the light on in her room at night. She was learning how to navigate her room in complete darkness. If she happened to go to school, she would do her homework on the tram on the way home. Life in the "field of cauliflowers" began to take shape. The bathing beauty's picture was on the front page of the *Herald* and Eadie's mother looked at it at the tea table. "Look at that, what next? If she was my daughter." And all the men nodded and smiled. They did not know that Eadie had cut her bathers up and now walked daily along the sand with the bathing beauty. Her bathers barely covered her. She had taken her old ones to the beach, the ones with the skirt that always got caught in her bum crack. The bathing beauty had a round knobby basket and from it came the knowledge of the world. The two child-girls sat under the pier on their towels. The bathing beauty showed her how to cut her bathers and make a two-piece. She had a small tin box with needles and thread and they sewed together to make wondrous things.

At home, Paddy was going through a bad patch. When Eadie took Nugget, the dog, for a walk, Mr Mott slunk along behind her and if she looked back, he would step behind a tree. Sometimes she gave him "the finger". The bathing beauty had taught her this when men followed the girls along the beach. She told her, "You only use this in special cases. It's not to be done all the time, it could work against you."

The bathing beauty had a very heavy accent. Eadie got hugged a lot by the bathing beauty and kissed on either side of the head every time they said goodbye or hello. She told the bathing beauty, "You have a beautiful language" and she didn't just mean when she talked.

When they walked along to Little Jerusalem, they both got hugged and kissed on either side of the head. The bathing beauty got greeted in all different languages and Eadie would ask, "What's that?" The bathing beauty would reply, "He's French." Or, "That's Yiddish." Or, "He's my father's partner in the business."

When the two girls sat on the wall that held back the sand from the lawn, a crowd gathered. Eadie listened to the talk. Elderly women brought up hats and suntan oil and rubbed the bathing beauty's shoulders. Eadie's, too, for she had become a bathing beauty as well. She ate the crusty bread cut in big heavy slices and liked her life a lot, despite a mother that was a dead loss.

When the bathing beauty took a hold on Eadie's

heart, she almost forgot about Mr Mott. When she was walking in the autumn leaves or bumping along in the tram absent-mindedly, he would suddenly be there, with his demonic fly-eyes. Argh! Firecrackers went off in that part of her brain that regulated fear. She tried to laugh at him. Paddy could not be approached on the subject of Mr Mott without a major, clench-fisted reaction. When the adults were out and Eadie was in the bath, she would see his face through the smoked, crinkled glass. The dog, Nugget, slept outside the bathroom window on the closed-in verandah. He liked Mr Mott. Mr Mott gave him pieces of Cadbury's milk chocolate.

Winter came, the beach was deserted, the bathing beauty went to Munich, and Eadie thought seriously about killing Mr Mott.

Legs

When winter came, Eadie joined the local athletics
club. She missed the bathing beauty, but her affec-
tions were claimed by another. She lived in Eadie's
street and went to the same school, which just
showed how hybrid safeties can journey into life
when reality gets too grim.

Everyone had always called this girl, Legs. In the
classroom, she irritated the teachers without excep-
tion. She took up too much space, spreading herself
across two desks, her splendid thighs flexed across
the aisle, her calves pink and muscled, ever ready for
the run. She told Eadie, "I gain strength from the
recuperating powers of the run."

She was tuned in to the integrity of the spirit. She
kept that spirit revitalised and stimulated with the legs
that never failed her. They defied limitations. Her
beautiful accomplished legs. Mysterious, honest, bold
legs. If she moved them in the classroom, recrossed, or
slightly flexed the ankle, the whole class was attentive.
Eyes would shift and edge down to the movement,
mesmerised. Mouths went dry, hearts beat faster.
Watching those legs brought relief from tension. Only
the teachers would be annoyed. Authoritative figures

came and went in the school but these legs resided in dreams. Eadie liked to look at her friend's face when she was running. It was the wind and the sea that she thought of when she saw her friend running in the distance.

There were beauties in the class, but no duplicate for the challenge Eadie felt when she saw her, bounding along in her lone marathon, all at once the most beautiful of all. Her huge angular feet mowing up grasses with her horselike stride, the large face thrown back in ecstasy.

The teachers used her as an example of the student who absorbed the least. She said, "I am an athlete, that is what I do." Eadie nodded in harmony. She was told that she wouldn't get a job or a husband. Negative advice abounded. She was given forecasts to propel her to despair.

She had virile shoulders, a long neck that swelled at the base. An image of forcefulness, but many thought her, at best, an ugly girl with long legs.

In the rural area that she came from, she often ran with her bold legs to the next town. She brought in her father's cows, her wonderful legs pumping the ground.

Eadie herself became a swift and enduring runner and hardly lost her breath. On Tuesday nights, she caught two trams to her Grandma Siddy's and stayed the night. It was not the same as the old days. There was no garden wall to sit against. Sometimes she went to Alice Wilt's at the weekend and they would play all the old songs. Eadie couldn't play music at home because Paddy was nervy. Every day she would run around the oval with Legs.

There was something contagious in the vitality of the run. They ran in the pitch-black night and in the storm winds along the beach. On sultry days, and late autumn ones, they practised long jumps and high jumps. They went to the indoor pool and practised diving. Eadie Wilt got a new pair of skirted bathers and hid the ones mutilated by the bathing beauty.

Paddy was looking for a serious "thing". Something deep and hurtful that could explain or end her pain. The *objet d'art* of her life was this search for the wildness within that ate her away. Eadie remembered the afternoons of her childhood, when her mother cut her hair and they sat out on the back steps and some-times made eye contact. Eadie got a shiver from those black eyes. The faraway distant greens of her own eyes reminded Paddy of the "bad seed" from which her daughter had sprung. Frankie Wilt had become buoyantly evil in a short space of time, and "you are just like him," she told Eadie. Criminal activities were hinted at. Eadie wondered if the concession ticket that he had arduously taught her to fake had anything to do with it. She had enjoyed that project a lot. Under plastic, you could not tell the difference. They had done it together when they were both at Grandma Alice's for the weekend. She had used it on the tram all term and the conductor never questioned its authenticity.

Eadie was labouring with Mr Mott who was becoming more and more sinister. He stalked her all the time now. Eadie had exams and had to leave her bedroom lights on to study. This meant that he could look all night. There were curtains which she pinned together but he always found a crack where he could see something; a foot, or an elbow.

When she was home alone, he became more aggressive. Locked out of the main house, he would peer in the window and tap on the pane. One rain-soaked afternoon, Eadie had her mother's box of photographs down, sitting on the floor with them spread out before her, in her mother's bedroom. This was forbidden and was Eadie's favourite pastime in her mother's house.

She saw Mr Mott go up and down a few times with his umbrella to the letterbox. He even knocked on the back door. She did not answer. He looked in the window and knocked on the pane. She did not look up, turning her back to the window. He did not keep up the pestering. He did not want to attract the attention of the neighbours.

The photographs created new beliefs and awaken-ings every time Eadie saw them; Joe Flood, in a sweatsoaked singlet, bending in a doorway, majest-ically transparent as the sun caught his back and shoulders as he eyed the camera. His reflection swirled in a dry universe, caught happy and ridiculous, straight-thighed and wind drunk. Eadie remembered Joe Flood well. She was revelling in the private pleasure of him. She thought of him, as in a communal sleep, wickedly dead, a polite distance from the living but still contactable.

A thunderstorm edged its way into the skies above the streets, and Mr Mott took himself back to his bungalow to wait. Inside the hatbox were newspaper clippings. There was a story here but she could not read it as a coherent whole. A picture of Paddy wearing gloves; Eadie knew the suit. It was powder-blue and Paddy had tailored it herself and everyone said it was a magnificent job. It was very out of fashion now, the wrong length and collar, but Paddy still had it hanging in the wardrobe with mothballs in the pockets. Eadie liked it. She tried it on when Paddy was out. She read the newspaper clippings and they said that Paddy Wilt was an exceptional designer. Paddy smiled beside a tall woman in a beaded dress that shimmered.

Eadie still went walking with the dog around the neighbourhood and met all sorts of people. She learnt the short cuts and she ran through the churchyard across the gravel. Mr Mott could not follow because the priest always sat there on his bench at this time of the evening. It looked bad if a man came running after a girl, right across the churchyard.

At night, he was at her window. It didn't matter how little he saw. One night she went to the bathroom, and while she was out of the room, he took the wire screen off and opened the window a few inches so that the breeze lifted the curtains now and then. He put the screen back on and settled back on his haunches. Eadie knew that she had pulled the window down. "*I must fix him,*" she thought. She went next day before school to make his bed. Her duties before school were bed-making and vacuuming. She was red-eyed that morning. She had lain awake fretting about this *Mott* man. She reached into his laundry basket and with revulsion caught a snotty handkerchief on a twig snapped from a tree at the door of his bungalow. Looking to the left and right for a suspicious Paddy, she carried this loathsome thing down the side of the house and placed it on the lawn outside her window. She knew he had already gone to work but she was frightened by what she had done. Desperate too. She went into the house and took her mother's arm and pulled her out of the house and down the side. Something broke, she sobbed and cried out uncontrollably as she pointed to the odious crumpled thing, knowing all the time she was setting the bloke up. Made no difference. The bastard was scaring her. Paddy, of course, gave her a clout and told her to get to school. She washed the handkerchief and replaced it in his room. Whether she had an opinion of how it got there or not, Eadie never knew. The dog followed Eadie all the way to the tram-stop and people stared because she was crying in her sleeve and looked more messy than ever.

He Came through the Door
in His Shirt Sleeves . . . Quickly

This was when Paddy got sick, around about then. The stalking of Eadie Wilt took a startling turn and the girl knew she would have to make a plan to get rid of this weird bugger. He began to act reckless, saying whatever he liked to her and taking risks. Whenever Eadie set the table, she would point all the knives in the direction of his place. She decided that she needed all the help she could get; omens and prayers and curses, whatever. He slid behind his newspaper and sometimes he'd kick her shins under the table. Eadie cried out and Paddy glared, her lips pressed tight.

This was the normal home life that Paddy had talked about during all those years in the pub with Grandma Siddy. You can stick it, thought Eadie as she walked along the canal, slipping through fence holes and walking through mucky places so that he would be as uncomfortable and dirty as possible. She turned around and saw his dark body solemnly moving under the trees. She turned into a friend's house and made a noisy journey down the sideway. He stood firmly near the bus stop. She wondered about his oddness. She was deciding on her own conspiracies. It took up all her time now. She went to visit Legs at her house; it did not appear strange or distorted. She wondered if the sounds were the same and the hiding places as easy to find. She went with her friend who offered to dink her on her bike. They wobbled past him.

"Isn't that your boarder?" asked Legs as she caught the forlorn smile of the creepy bloke as they passed him sitting at the bus stop.

"Does he still give you Mars Bars?" asked her friend innocently, not knowing that he was clutching one now. They went on the wobbly bike to the oval to perfect their jumps. Eadie forgot her problems with Mr Mott and ran a few laps and hung upside down from the monkey bars.

When she arrived home, Paddy had a migraine and Eadie had to squash her effervescent feeling so as not to antagonise her. She felt so good she gave off explosive little laughs of energy. Paddy went to bed vomiting into a bucket, walking to the bathroom, all bent up. Mr Mott turned his haunted little face up to Eadie as she served him mashed potato. After she finished the dishes, she took Paddy a cup of tea. She sat on the edge of her mother's bed and looked into the scared, harrowed face. She saw a very big afraidness; so whole and great a terror she never saw again in all her life. Where did it come from? What could she do? Her mother was silent but something cried out. A telegraphed tear squeezed out through the dark eyes. Demure sobs, clutching at the throat, rushed out strangled. Eadie wrapped her smallish arms around the bedjacket and pressed her lips into the hair. The smell dashed her senses. This was a different breed of love. She breathed in her mother with deep unattractive sniffs. She stayed holding delicately and rocked with maternal determination. She must look after this mother, this new dark mother who smelt like this and was hers. Paddy was too sick to bitch, and complimented the good tea. Eadie smoothed the bed and washed Paddy's face with a warm face-washer. She hung around fussing for the newly loved mother until Paddy got fed up and pissed her off, so she could sleep.

That night, Eadie made a glue of flour and water and pasted newspapers over her window, three layers thick. When they dried, they could not be removed. No one could see in or out of that window. She left the light on until very late. Before she fell asleep, she said two firm prayers: one for Paddy; the other, said with wild speed, was a deal with God, and it concerned Mr Mott. Speaking with a child's calm, pure-hearted, she asked God if he might take him "up there" very soon, somewhat peacefully, without malice. Before she could offer something in return, the dark wave of sleep rolled into her chest and the deal was left half done, but still, she supposed God knew what she wanted.

Next afternoon, Paddy went to the doctor. Eadie helped her to get dressed. The house was strange and silent. It was a weekday, no one was there on weekdays, and Eadie had stayed home from school to help her mother.

Eadie sat on the carpet looking at a photograph. Paddy with a short haircut in a shimmering dress. Eadie sat quietly on her heels, humming to herself. She did not hear the doornob turn.

Suddenly, He came through the doorway in his shirtsleeves . . . quickly. The obvious fright that followed stayed indelibly with her for a long time. The man had never laid a hand on her before, though she was scared enough of him anyway. He was there, coming from nowhere. He lifted her by the throat, his hands around her neck, lifting her up to his face. Eadie could hear the thornbush tapping on the window. A weary, wistful fury shuddered through the house as he swayed her to and fro by her throat, with her little legs dangling. He rubbed her face against his and she felt saliva running down her cheeks. He spoke in a halting, gentle voice that he used only to her, clutching at her neck and waving her around like a rag. Paddy's special things went flying from her lap all around the room. She understood that her mother could not protect her. He gave Eadie a small punch in her stomach and the child saw the nastiness, hoarded up, tumble out of him. He sent her flying on to her mother's bed, so perfectly made. This place did not seem like earth. This hurtling embittered place. He stretched in a savage yawn and turned desperately when he heard a car pull into the yard. Eadie was largely overcome; he warned her, "I am a force to be reckoned with," he said. The vigorous girl held her mother's lamp in her hand, having regained her senses. She heard him say, "I am a force."

She wept, her mind crowded with distress. He went out of the room, to the front door, and closed it behind him as Paddy and Hardy entered from the back yard. Eadie felt as if she was emptying all over her mother's bed. Paddy went berserk, at the room and its contents, so strewn about. Mostly, from the "lies" that she was hearing from this difficult child.

"Why are you doing this?" she asked her daughter, who was sitting in a heap, with her boots leaving marks all over the sheets. Hardy carried Eadie away. She was having an impact on him. She softened and cried into his shoulder.

"He came in and punched me and tried to choke me." Hardy rocked her, consoling as best he could.

"The door's locked, darl," he said softly, "And Nugget's there. He wouldn't let him in, would he?"

It was predictable. He was reasonable. He spent a lot of time and energy figuring it all out. He even went out to the bungalow and snooped around. He didn't have much time for the fellow; he'd met weird codgers before in Turkey, during the war, especially.

Summer was coming around again. Eadie once more went to the beach via the storm-water drains, looking out for the bathing beauty. It was a dicey time for Eadie. Her mother kept tricking her, turning inside out. She had come home one afternoon and her mother lay pale and seized with pain. She lay half out of the bed and wheezed to Eadie to lift her. Eadie held her in fright and her mother stiffened in pain. Eadie felt an extraordinary despair; she quivered as she laid her mother's frail and exposed body back on the bed, in the beam of sunlight. She looked defenceless. Their hands touched and a violent shuddering quickened through Paddy, and Eadie was breathless. The ambulance came and took her away and they removed things at the hospital, mostly bits of body. During that time, Hardy was always at the hospital with Paddy. Eadie had to make the beds and clean before school. At night, she served the dinners and did the washing up. She locked the back door and had a bath. Mr Mott would be hanging out his washing on the line. He looked pathetic and agitated. He's darkening the day again, she said to God, still waiting for a sign. In fits and snatches, he worked himself into a state of plaintive behaviour. Sometimes Eadie walked into his bungalow to make his bed and he would be fumbling with himself. The beads of sweat on his forehead floated down his face and dripped off his chin.

"I'll come back later," she would say, and she'd have to shake him off. The smell of him. Sometimes just making his bed could make her go and have another shower just to get rid of the smell.

There were places he did not follow her to. School was one such place. It was foreign to him, she thought. He did not know about her wagging school either. Once she was off the tram and near the school gate, everything was right. He followed the tram sometimes, but never after a certain point. When she changed trams, he never followed the second tram. He went off to work, to his own world, and left her alone. It was a triumph, really; wagging school. It wasn't that she hated school; no, she loved it. When she began writing stories, they were often about school, but not going to school gave her great promise. She could choose and control her life, and do any of a number of things.

So this day, she pulled things together at home, caught the school tram with the boy with the red hair, swapped sandwiches with him and walked the drains to the beach. There were no people on the beach. She put her school dress in the plastic bag with the drawstring and swam out to her boat. She never thought of who owned it; it had been hers for so long. She plunged down into the water, tasting the good salt. She dived into the jellyfish and then lay in the sun. She was fatigued, and struggled with daydreams that had a nightmarish quality. She peered out to sea, and the boat rolled and scooped up water. A murmur filled her ears. Some miseries paralysed her, every now and then, spoiling the fun, but she did sleep. For hours and hours.

She woke up suddenly, and the heat of the sun was blind and indifferent. She felt a shadow over her and saw a dark shape, cruel and grimy, covering her. It overwhelmed her in a conventional way; inventing itself from every fear she ever had, embellished and wretched. A rush of vileness pondering on and taking shape from her childish notion of evil. It was a disappointing setback, this fabulous daydream of evil, the taste of it obliged her to be bolder in her commands to God. She felt impelled to insist. She caught the tram home and thought about Mr Mott; she might have to kill him. She became very dramatic and said that while the man was around her, the world was sunless, skyless, starless.

When her mother was in the hospital, Mr Mott tested her endurance to the hilt. He came to the bathroom window and pushed his face against the glass. She had long given up trying to enlist Hardy. He was not a believer. Her mother would be coming home in the next few days. She checked around the back yard to see who was home and listened at Mott's bungalow door for the sound of his radio. Nothing. She started to run a bath and passed between her room and the bathroom several times. Steam filled the room and came out into the passage. She was alerted to the window now; the glass was covered by the collage of newspapers. She thought she saw the curtain move as she was passing the crack in the half-open door. She stared through the crack and stopped dead when she saw two hands come past the curtains to hold them back. The steam was all around her. The sound of the water was loud, crashing from the taps. He had taken the screens from the window. How had he opened the window? She moved with weightless legs on bare feet out of the front door and down the block to the house where Legs lived. The girl was on the grass in the dark yard, cross-legged, rolling her dog around. Eadie slashed through the grasses. Breathless. She only made an arm motion to follow, nothing more. Legs twisted expertly upright and brazenly leaned into a run. Neither of them spoke until they rounded the bend of Eadie's bedroom on the bungalow side of the house.

Slags, Bitches, Sluts and More

As they sped under starry skies, through the suburban night, it occurred to Eadie that God was probably not the "old he" as she had always believed. The two girls were off to make things right without help or malice. Eadie felt wise and strong and thought of the rapturous maidens, wind-brave and stealth-hearted, that Grandma Siddy told stories about. She looked at her friend and kept her eyes on her as they moved across the grasses towards that exhausted face at the window, around the corner, under the tree. They skidded to a standstill as they beheld him, silly as anything, naked to the knee, holding his dick with socks all wet from the dew. His hair was shaggy and frayed, and the jerking of his head made his chin rest on his chest. Legs took two giant leaps, landing in his face. Her glorious humungous thighs were shining and pumping adrenalin through the tight knots of her fierce muscles. Neck and shoulders, swollen and sinewy, strained in a massive sigh of exasperation.

The exorcism that took place shook the smothering silence for a panicky moment. A high-pitched screech foamed from the man and sent them right off balance.

"Slags! Bitches! Sluts!" he undulated in a crippled

voice, while pandemonium hammered out from the kicking, punching bloke. Slags, bitches, sluts, he called them, and more. His crazy static craving to be heard degenerated as the foam, in voluminous gushes from his mouth, stuffed up his whole speech. Eadie watched in awful wonder. His hands waved like a metronome. Legs spoke in conciliatory tones, but he was suddenly furious and wrenched at her head, tearing in desperation. He was slicing and gouging at the big girl who all the time spoke very low as he barked out and hissed with excruciating self-pity. Finally, Legs flipped him over with a powerful ankle and jostled him to the ground. She had him down; his naked bottom was covered in mud. He was somehow now in communication. Legs hauled herself on him and he laughed and she laughed with him. His eyes blazed and there was much panting and holding of breath before the bargaining began.

The man was wanting this confrontation to be over. He was back to normal and thinking straight.

"Please get off me," he said breathlessly. He was summing up his possibilities. He was thinking that he had better devise new rules. Legs murmured into his face: "Try to listen."

He opened his mouth but nothing came, in answer.

"You are leaving this house."

He started with his slow smile, but something savage and threatening, almost disordered, disturbed him about the girl sitting on him. The schizophrenic coldness in the girl's astonishing face floated to its target. He was feeling threatened enough to stare and listen. The bad-dream quality of the night was snuffing out his competence. His sinuses were bad. He felt the worms and water seeping up through the ground. The reproachful silent night was perfecting his downfall. He burst into tears.

The lights from the Cohns' house next door came on and Mrs Cohn called from her back door. "Who is that? Is anyone there?"

Eadie answered. "It's just the dog Mrs Cohn! After the chickens. Sorry. It's all right now."

That they had no chickens, Mrs Cohn would never know. The three stood now, cold angels under a bare tree; the echoes of their pact dragging them in all directions. The girls started to walk off, leaving him standing there, his blind pink dick flaccid and mute for all to see. Except there was only Eadie and Legs and they didn't care to look any more.

"Leave this house or I'll have you locked up," Legs told him. It was a workable threat. One that could be believed, but Eadie did not think it would work at all. Tonight he had that mad sad face, with the moon's rays leaking down on him. His mouth was agape with self-pity, but tomorrow he would wake up new and refreshed and he would continue with his muck. Eadie felt as if she was made of water. Dark sounds came from her; she wasn't going to get rid of him after all.

The girls reached the turning of the wall and Legs picked up the tennis racquet that she had grabbed when they had begun their mercy run, what seemed like hours ago. Actually, it had only taken five minutes to do all this. The shadows ached across the garden as the girls were about to leave him.

"Sluts. Cunts," he hissed, feeling more confident. He had decided he could deny all of this. No one would believe Eadie's simple friend, especially his landlady. The night roared. Legs made a sweeping, low, curving jump. A bird-cry, beautiful with light, caught the tender night air. Eadie remembered the whiteness of the legs as they hit the ground. The crack of sound, and hands braced for a fall as the tennis racquet swept back and caught his skull in a hard blue bolt of shock. The lullaby of hurt, and now, terrible oaths of serious promise from the girl clinched the deal. He suddenly agreed that it was time he was leaving.

"It was a dream and does not mean a thing," she told Eadie, who was now highly distressed. The wide eye, a flat blind tint of life, the sallow bald spot on his head, was scratched with blood. He was beginning to remember their differences. Tap tap tap went his heart at this great event, patient to keep him alive. His ears were ringing and he was flattened and lurid and everything seemed clear.

Eadie then took her bath, and Legs sat on the side in her bright yellow jumper. Mr Mott was in his bungalow and the lawn outside Eadie's window was raked and the flywire screen replaced. The girls were putting things right in their clandestine way. They felt good together; a feeling of total belonging. All the tangible dangers seemed shifted and less fearful when they were together.

The next few weeks were rough, however. Mr Mott played cat and mouse. Paddy came home from hospital stricken. She was trying to retrieve her life, but she never did get it back. She was upset and not too talkative. Eadie tried to pursue the questions of the operation. She wanted to help fix everything for Paddy. She let the child kiss her but mostly she shut herself away and knitted cardigans, breathing shallowly and crouching against the fat pillows with her high arched eyebrows dark and, against great odds, lush and rich and beautiful.

Hardy stayed home from work to look after things. Eadie decided to do everything by the book. She went to school and came home at four o'clock in the afternoon.

"Sit with Mum," Hardy would say.

The fire would be lit in the sitting room next to Paddy's bedroom, and she would be there by the fire in her faded men's pyjamas with her knitted dressing-gown around her shoulders. She looked absolutely whipped but could tolerate Eadie's overcloseness. This was Eadie's favourite episode with her mother, who sometimes cried in pain, from lack of air or tiredness.

"I am going to the unknown, Eadie, and I'm not coming back."

This did not frighten Eadie. She felt that that was where she was going herself. She looked forward to it. She kissed and cuddled her mother all the time, and Paddy did not say much. Hardy brought their tea in on a tray and they ate together by the fire.

Eadie had unreliable memories of this time. Mr Mott was making her nervous by not leaving. It helped that she did not have to eat at the table every night. Hardy was a little icy to him and supported Eadie in her dislike of the man. After two weeks had gone by, the obvious enemy was still very much part of the house. Now he bought little gifts for Paddy and came into her room and sat by the fire, under the pretext of presenting his flowers or books to the patient.

On the final day, when Eadie was feeling most traumatised, Legs came to collect her for the athletics club. Mr Mott had just bought all the Sunday newspapers for Paddy and was standing at the fire smiling down on her. Legs came in the back door and asked Hardy about Paddy. He liked to talk to this girl. They shared a country outlook. Without warning, the girl began to testify to other evils besides the injustices of their suburbs. It was most unexpected.

"I'm glad your wife's getting better now," she said.

He strained to pick up the meaningful in her attempts to explain the situation.

"I'm going to the authorities about your boarder, Mr Mott," she said in her matter-of-fact voice, "Is he still here?"

With some elegance and brevity, she told him all she knew about the raw deal that they had made with

Mott. He took her to Paddy's room, where Mr Mott smiled into the fire. Hardy burst in rather animatedly.

"Legs has something you should hear, Paddy."

He glared uncharacteristically at Mr Mott with such hostility that the man knew the game was up. He stammered and suddenly made gestures that were incompatible with the design and order of the room.

"Oh, well, I'd better be going. I just wanted to tell you that I have to give my notice. One week . . . if that's all right."

It was garbled and sparse and steeped in confusion because he hadn't planned to be doing it at all. He was incapable of coherent thought, but Paddy looked suspicious, which meant she really was much better. Hardy followed him out and took down his suitcases with no sympathy.

"Pack up," he said, and it was enough.

Mr Mott didn't sleep another night. The unspoken message was that Hardy was extremely sincere in wanting him gone.

The shell exploded. It was Paddy's anger at now having one of her bungalows empty with no paying tenant. She supected Eadie, and it was enough to get her well and truly on her feet again. She did not show her scars to Eadie any more, and no kissing and cuddling took place by the fire. When Eadie saw that Paddy was looking pissed off, she was glad because she knew everything was back to normal.

Little Things that Hang Down

He was not a wise or educated man. Apart from that which every general practitioner must know, he knew nothing.

The only remarkable thing about the morning had been this child who, while having her twisted knee looked at, had dropped her underpants, spread her stoic legs and asked, "What is this little thing that hangs down?" She looked perplexed and shielded her eyes from the morning sun that flooded the room and made them both squint. He wasn't about to tell her, not just like that, anyway. She wanted concrete detail. Was it all right? Had it come loose from some other part of her anatomy?

His was an old-fashioned practice. His rooms still had the air of silent foetuses in bottles floating in the light. He shrank from the subversive child, calling the nurse. He wasn't going to start talking about clitorises or any other genital for that matter. Not with a full waiting room.

Legs and Eadie found out anyway. From a book. They compared and explored, and decided that each was the same but different. Each had its own kind of appeal. They called them their clits and supposed that thousands of other young girls did the same.

Enormous vanity and curiosity had surfaced in the two girls since they had, with some glory, rid themselves of Mr Mott. The nightmarish thing was that Eadie had begun to feel sorry for him. In retrospect, they had discussed the occurrence many times and the propaganda had worn a bit thin. Eadie now remembered good things about him. It was Siddy Church's fault. "Everyone has something very good," she'd say. They picked over the bones of the Mott memory and decided that he did have a beautiful singing voice. He sang in the choir and his voice had such great despair and scriptural resonance that one could not believe ill of one whose voice, with crystalline purity, lamented the wretched sins of the congregation. His legacy to Legs and Eadie was a record album left in his room. In his hurried departure, he had missed it.

"Throw it out," said Paddy.

Eadie took it to Legs' house and they played it on the record player. It had songs there with names like "Weep No More", "Sad Fountains", and "Wilt Thou, Unkind, Thus Reave Me of My Heart". A mixture of poem, melody and harmony, treble and bass viols, flutes, lute, cittern and bandore, and a miraculous singer. Both girls were spellbound. Legs asked, "What sort of singer is he?"

They read the record cover: "Alfred Deller, countertenor" and, "the spirit sings free from the weight of the flesh". Eadie had never read a truer word. It just proved what Siddy Church had said. "Just about everyone has something to teach you, if you'll only look and listen."

From Mr Mott, who gave her a bad time, she received this inspiration, this voice from another universe. She knew the songs off by heart and tried to mimic the miracle. Nature had not been generous in this regard, and Paddy would give her a resounding clout if she ever heard "Wilt Thou, Unkind, Thus Reave Me of My Heart".

"You'll reave me of my sanity," said Paddy, her gulled eyebrows flapping with irritation.

Legs and Eadie ran around like lovers. In the world of girlfriends, they were loyal lovers. They high-jumped and ran the oval backwards just to be stupid. School was another universe, one that Eadie was very interested in. Legs was withdrawn and tended to disappear into the background. It didn't change their relentless interest in each other. Legs let her go her own way, always asking questions and causing a stir and upsetting the teachers.

Eventually, Eadie lost Legs for a while. She left school and went to Sydney to work in the Leagues Clubs. Eadie heard that she had married. Someone she worked with, at least twice her age. He fell in love with the swaggering, ravishing thing that Eadie knew so well. If you saw it, it seized you, thought Eadie. He recklessly lost his head and left his wife and children. In their pursuit for the new and pure, they went to live in a remote country district. It was not an inventive technique for surefire happiness, but their fascination for the opposite in each other kept them healthily intimate for a good many years. The child-bride's physical audacity dominated the marriage. She had captured all his imagination, every square inch of it. They lived for a half decade and farmed and loved well and continuously until a gloomy entombing miscalculation turned everything around.

Eadie had contacted Legs and, after several letters, had made the long and arduous train trip to the haven of her friend. If contentment could be measured, all happiness Eadie herself had ever felt would fall into oblivion. This quality was unsettling; this communicating of absolute and effortless contentment.

It went on and Legs had a child, though she was still herself a child. She wrote that she worked now as a teacher at the country school. She taught arithmetic and physical training. The surrounding farmers liked her. They often saw her running with their children in a cross-country run. Her husband, Sam, stayed home on the land that they bought and he began to build their farmhouse. They had a tractor and a horse and an orchard of fine young trees. When Eadie went to stay, they fussed and spoilt her rotten and never wanted her to leave. Eadie liked Sam because Sam loved Legs. Sometimes, they told Sam the story of Mr Mott. He said it was as gripping as an airport thriller. Sam liked to smoke joints a lot. Eadie had an aversion to men who smoked joints all day. Legs told her she was sounding like Paddy. If anything could cause

Eadie to reverse her opinions or behaviour, it was this timely information.

Of course, in the time of Legs and Eadie and Mr Mott, no one had heard of joints, not in that neighbourhood. Not until the 1960s had lifted their skirts to reveal a shock of pubic hair did the intricate little devices of drugs consort easily with the minutiae of ordinary experience. People were still getting used to Brigitte Bardot and Elvis. Eadie did not have to try to be different. Paddy provided her with very weird clothes, black fake-fur jackets and other odd numbers from the fantasyland of her mother's wardrobe. Eadie had little resistance to her dressing. People stared at her on the tram when she went ice skating on Saturdays with Legs. The boys that went to the Jewish school called her the black widow spider. She turned heads wherever she walked; the hair-raising gothic of her black velvets contrasted vividly with the other girls on the tram stop, in their peachy dresses with seamed stockings and white pointed shoes. Her baby face was shameless and certain. It was not a good look. One day she was standing on the corner of St Moritz and a man asked her the time. The paddy wagon screeched by and three cops jumped out.

"What's your name? How old are you? Does your mother know you're here in the worst part of St Kilda?"

They put her in the van and drove around for hours, then took her back to St Kilda police station where a policewoman searched and questioned her.

Was she a runaway? The man who asked her the time was a known criminal. Did she know that?

"Not to me, he wasn't!" said Eadie with some elegance.

"We could charge you with consorting," the policewoman said, without a taint of wellmeaningness. It was another of those occasions when Legs came to the rescue. She was to meet Eadie on the tram stop. Finding her missing, she asked around and came presently to the police station, bestowing dignity with her striding athletic presence. She spoke up for Eadie, formal as a sonnet, tall and grown-up, extracting admiration for her loins, so strong and self-contained. Eadie was saved again, and they went out into the night with their arms around each other. In the world of girlfriends, they were loyal lovers.

When they were adults, though everything had changed, Legs and Eadie, the early versions, kept on. Walk beside them, even when things got grim, and you stopped believing in every bloody thing.

After Legs had one strong and beautiful son, she went back to work at the local school. The farmhouse was always a meeting place for people. The green smoky air of the valley intoxicated Eadie on those rare occasions when she went to visit.

Legs had a second son and went back to work again. Sam looked after the boys and worked the farm, building and fencing, and frigging around with his tractor. Legs told Eadie, she couldn't believe her luck. She was rolling a joint and ran her tongue along the paper and her inner light blazed out of her like so much neon.

Eadie heard much later what had happened. Sam had driven his tractor to the gate. The baby was perched in the bucket seat. Sam pulled on the brake and went to the gate to open it. The baby smiled and sat very still. He was used to this procedure. No one dared say what happened. If the baby touched the brake no one knew. The tractor rolled forward. Sam's sky fell in. He ran like a horse, his blood flooding his arteries, his throat. He felt weightless, he was nothing. His boy toppled backwards into the grader, hitched to the back of the tractor, and nothing was ever the same again.

At the hospital, Eadie heard that Sam promised God he would devote every minute of his life to the boy if he would let him live. Everyone murmured to themselves, No, God. No. The story told was that the nurses had already heard "the last breathing"; that particular rhythm that heralds the final breath.

When Legs was told that her boy was in a coma, she did not believe it, any more than she believed he was blind and did not hear anything. He looked like an angel, unmarked and perfect. She saw him as being "locked up". Or "stuck" and would come out of it, awash with curiosity after a long sleep. She would wrap him up and run with him across the hills in the wondrous smoky air, her miraculous legs mowing up the grasses. She whispered all the sweeter oaths and promises that she believed in.

The doctors had said that he would not come out of the coma. They shrugged when he did. Sam and Legs sat on the couch with him, both cradling the precious "saved". Legs was no longer the child-bride. She looked older than her older husband; he was old inside. Everything had seized up around his heart.

There came a time when no one noticed those legs any more. Her other strengths eclipsed the visible muscle power of her beautiful wayward limbs.

The broken baby grew and grew, despite those who advised Legs that he would die quickly. He'll never sit, walk, see, swim, speak, know or fathom out the world. He'll always be a burden, a drain, a boy of no use whatsoever. He came out of his coma and opened wide blue eyes that did not and would not ever see, said the doctors.

"He sees colours," said Legs, "and that's enough for now."

They took him to every specialist, therapist and quack that their money would allow. Never, never, never, said everyone.

"He's waiting for his miracle. See? He's listening for it."

People shook their heads at the gallant fool of a woman. She did not give in; she read books, wrote letters to government offices pestering them for a treatment centre in their remote area. She wrote to other parents with special children like hers. She had to go back to work when the money ran out. Their elder, perfect son lost slices of his childhood. He went to school each day with Legs. Sam made a little cart and harnessed the baby into place. He pushed him around the farm while he worked. They knew he could hear, because he turned his head if he heard birds or his father's voice. One day he made a humming noise when Sam was playing with him and changing his nappy. He was a huge baby by this time. They expected that he would always need to wear a nappy. They had their routine. Sam would get Legs off to work and then take him into the bath. He had made a great big bathtub with cement and tiles; a small swimming pool. He would lower the boy in and then hop in with him and float him around and exercise his legs, making them imitate a kicking motion.

"There's nothing wrong with the legs," said the specialist. "It's the signal box, the main switchboard, that's gone bung! It's a pity he fell into that grader headfirst; we might still have something to work with."

As the father dried and fastened his nappy, he felt a vibration in the chest. A chill exhilaration came over the man. He stopped dead. From a far-off forgotten tunnel, a small breeze echoed up and up until the walls caught the humming and bounced it around like some unearthly singsong. Sam cried and laughed and made jokes that were mutely accepted by the humming boy. It was the first communication. He did it when he was pleased or comfortable. He hummed during and after a bath. A new nappy pleased him and when Legs came home at night, a cacophony of sound, like many bees swarming, greeted her.

The elder son went to the school with his mother. The two at home forged an existence that was more or less happy. To the outside world, it was a living tragedy.

He could flail his arms around and he could lift them to his right eye. Something was irritating him in that eye. He would grow very agitated and claw at his right eye. They tied padded gloves on him to stop him hurting himself. He twisted and scowled noiselessly and, in frustration, his hands banged the front bar of his harness. He lifted himself out of the harness. He's telling me something, thought Sam. Maybe he wants to be changed. He changed him and the humming began. This is how Sam said he talked to him. He also chuckles. But no one else had heard that except Legs.

Sam spent every waking hour with his son just as he said he would. The plan had to be modified quickly when one day Sam himself threw a fit. It was bewildering. He keeled over, frothed and foamed, bit through his tongue. Worst still, he shat himself and dropped the boy and rolled on top of him. It was Saturday and Legs was in the garden.

"Did you know he was epileptic?" the doctor asked Legs. "It's the pressure," he continued, when she did not answer.

Legs stayed at home and was up at daybreak to milk and farm, and harness the boy.

"This is the worst time of all," she wrote to Eadie Wilt.

Sam was knocked down and something horrible was waking up inside her son. He could not tell about it, but he banged his head like never before. He did not hum or buzz anymore.

"I think he will die soon," said Legs. "The miracles are drying up."

Eadie Wilt caught the five o'clock bus that drove all night. At seven next morning, she was at her friend's kitchen table, holding on her lap a giant quivering boy in padded gloves with sky-coloured eyes that did not see. He twisted and strained with tormented tugs and it was hard to hold him.

Legs' hair had gone a dirty grey, though she was not old. The house held the stench of tangible misery, or perhaps their strategies had to change. She carried the boy outside in the warm air. He was heavy, so she laid him down on the grass and loosened his clothes. He still seemed distressed, and banged and pounded with his head in a slow fury. Sometimes he stopped and listened.

Eadie and Legs walked around the land. It was peaceful out in the open spaces of paddocks. All Legs talked about was her son. She spoke as if she only had one son, the hurt one. She was locked into the subject and gave no thought to her other son, the one she neglected because of his wholeness. Eadie helped the older boy chop wood and carry it inside. She gave him cuddles when she could disguise it because he was not used to it.

That night, Legs and Eadie fell asleep by the fire.

Eadie kept waking up and listening to the low moans coming from her friend. Eadie stared at the familiar face and saw it had gone through a transition since the days of Mr Mott and "the little things that hang down". Legs woke and they looked at each other with old eyes that remembered everything at once.

"I'm up shit creek without a paddle," whispered Legs, and they locked limbs and cried wholeheartedly for all the messes of the world.

"I almost forgot, I have something for you," said Eadie, feeling custard-hearted and horrendously flowery all of a sudden. She crawled around trying to find her bag.

"Here it is, it's a record!" She went to the player and put it on the turntable. The celestial tones of crystalline yearning filled the room. Leg's inner lights shone out like so much neon.

"It's bloody old Alfred Deller," she yelled, "Mr Mott's record. Mr Bloody Mott's countertenor!"

Even Sam woke up and marvelled. They played both sides and got drunk on cooking sherry in the sober house. The children slept through all the racket, and next day Eadie left to go home. Eadie had brought the record because she knew that Legs had named her second son after Alfred, the countertenor, and she wanted her to hear those ravishing vibrations again. That voice comes from another place, thought Legs. As she changed her Alfred, she reached across and started the turntable. Eadie was gone and she felt a readiness to weep at any minute. She sat him in his harness and he started his tormented banging and Legs felt a grieving cry sweep through her. She cried easily and ceaselessly and, all through her crying, he twisted and distorted in silent fitful convulsions. When Legs felt relieved, she sighed and started anew like she always did. She lifted the needle onto the record and sank back and closed her eyes. She listened to "No More Sad Fountains" and did not hear the banging any more. She stayed on the couch for an hour until the final strains of "Wilt Thou, Unkind, Thus Reave Me of My Heart". She was smiling and listened because the last resounding note had faded but she could still hear something. A humming, like bees swarming.

"It's a miracle," she wrote to Eadie, "he loves Alfred Deller. He hums and coos as well."

Eadie wrote a card, "Little things that hang down and come loose from the anatomy of the past."

"What's she talking about?" asked Sam.

Was It 1956?
When Childhood Ended and Eadie Wanted to be Jewish

Eadie Wilt's childhood was slipping away. Television had come to Melbourne. People spent hours waiting for the test pattern to change on Channel Nine. The Olympic Games came in the same year and the coverage had the highest rating. Of course, it did. It was the only thing on.

She met a boy on the corner of the street; they were watching the aftermath of a car accident, everyone did that in 1956. His first words were: "Is that your dog?" She didn't answer. When she knew he wasn't looking, she gave a drowsy sideways glance. Very sly and leery and most unattractive, her mother told her every time she saw her doing it. He was predominantly red and yellow, with white-hooded eyes and pale blue iris centres. His nose was hooked; he looked alien, exotic and dangerous. He bent forward and lurched along, and his eyes narrowed before he spoke. His clothes were androgynously soft, the cardigan asked to be touched. Angora, or something, thought Eadie. His spidery eyelashes lay on his cheek when he looked down; everyone noticed his long white feathery lashes.

She was often at the mailbox when he rode by. His bike hurtled along all over the footpath. People went speechless for a moment, when they saw him.

"He looks like neither a boy or a girl," said Paddy. Eadie Wilt secretly thought he looked like a sea anemone; freckled blotches covered his face and arms. He radiated colour and light. He tossed his red hair and curls clung to his ears. He began to stop his bike whenever he saw Eadie Wilt. Sometimes in the morning they sat next to each other on the sixty-nine tram. They swapped sandwiches. Hers were Vegemite and egg, and his were black bread and weird fishes. Salami, dill pickles, herring and cold schnitzel. He never wagged school; he was a top student.

"Where were you?" he would ask. "Did you go to school today?"

She told him about swimming out to the boat and drifting at sea for the day. He got a different look in his eyes; curled up against her and his red-gold hair touched her cheek. She was occupied with watching Mr Mott weaving in and out of the traffic behind the tram, trying to get closer. It was in the time that she was still working out her plan with God to take him off her hands.

He liked the way she expressed herself. He was sharply aware of her lips and her command of her own poetry. She was very used to this beautiful boy by now. He was ahead of her in feelings, and he was always shaken up and slightly sick in his stomach when he saw her. He told her that he had mostly lived alone with his mother and grandmother. Eadie related well to this. She was always on the lookout for other mothers and grandmothers. They walked down the length of Lumeah Road, taking their time.

"I've got to get dinner on," she broke off at last and disappeared into her house. People liked to follow her, he thought, as he walked the half block that separated their houses. His mother had only recently remarried. He had wanted his mother to marry the man who owned the Arnott Biscuit factory. She had married, instead, the brother of her sister's husband. Now the two brothers from the smallgoods business were married to the two Wesoloski sisters from Berlin. His old grandmother, Anna Wesoloski, lived with them. He only saw his mother's new husband for twenty minutes each night during the evening meal. The rest of the time, he pretended he did not exist. The only other living relative he knew about was Auntie Charlotte. She was the sister of his dead father. He knew his father had gone broke making model airplanes at his button factory.

"He was messing around when he should have been making the buttons."

This was what his mother told him when he wasn't getting A's at school.

Anna Wesoloski saw Eadie Wilt from the front window and she liked the look of her, at least as much as her grandson did. One day, the boy came out of his house flanked by his mother and grandmother.

"Come and have some cake," they chorused in their heavy accents, and took her in. Every time she passed, they would call out: "Have some cake."

"Have some more cake." "Your mother doesn't feed you or what?"

That was how Eadie Wilt fell in love with these other mothers. They stayed loving and eating more cake for a good many years. Of course, one by one, they died, long after all the houses were pulled down and no one heard of them, any more.

They came from other places, and Eadie soon knew more about those places than she did her own.

When she was not roaming around with Legs, she would be down at her flame-haired friend's house, listening to his grandmother.

"How is Eadie Wilt today?" the old woman would ask, but it sounded like "Vilt" and Eadie liked that.

"I'm very fine and how is Anna Wesoloski?"

The old lady laughed hoarsely and began right in with talking. Eadie knew all of Anna Wesoloski's stories within a few months.

Sometimes she went swimming with Gertrude, Anna's daughter who was Gerald's mother. "I wish she was my mother," she told Gerald, "you're lucky to have a mother like that."

She told him she hated her mother. She even told Gertrude that she hated her mother.

"What! You hate your mother? *Meshuga Kvvutch*! Nobody can hate their mother. You are seeing me hate my mother?" And she took Eadie Wilt's face in her hands and sucked a kiss. Her mother, Anna Wesoloski, using the vacuum cleaner in the front room, came out to put in her bit.

"Sometimes blood is family and sometimes it is not."

Gertrude was often on the phone to someone called Charlotte. This was her sister-in-law from her first marriage. Her present husband had no patience for Charlotte. She had escaped Auschwitz by a few days. How she had got to England, she never said, but she had spent the war years there. In the bomb shelters, she entertained her captive audiences with witty literary repartee. She criticised Nietzsche and had cross-dressed in Berlin before the war. Gertrude had sepia photographs of her in lesbian groups; Charlotte in bold leather shorts standing astride or sitting neatly in a double-breasted suit.

"What is Auschwitz?" Eadie asked. She was hearing many new words and this was one of them. She went every day to Gertrude's house.

"Call me Mum," Gertrude said shyly.

"If you would like it. I'm going to run away from home," Eadie Wilt said. She was counting the days to her next birthday.

"What are you saying, *mina kleina galiptus puppen*? Here, have some schnitzel and boiled potatoes."

Eadie Wilt ate them and told her she would call her "Morma" and that she would call her "Morma" until the day she died. Gertrude thought her a dramatic child. Sometimes Eadie left her a note on the back door and it was addressed to "My Dear Morma", with an "r", the way it sounded.

Gertrude worked at a cake shop in Acland Street, a

few doors down from Scheherazade. Eadie would go there in her school uniform on her way home.

"Come with me, I drive you home, but first I must take these things to Charlotte."

They went to visit Charlotte. She had rooms in the back of an old mansion in Caulfield. She recognised a ready listener in Eadie. She was small and hunched, no neck to speak of, and gremlin hands twisted and arthritic. A tiny Greta Garbo face and white cotton-wool hair, though not much of it. She was famous around Melbourne.

"Have you read my letters to the editor in the *Age*?" She told Eadie Wilt that her nose had been used in an advertising campaign.

"'This Is a Jew's Nose'. That was me. The profile on those Nazi posters," she cackled importantly. "I was a poster queen."

Gertrude sniffed and unpacked the groceries, while Charlotte snapped nonstop questions.

"What do you think of that?"

She wanted everyone to speak up.

"Well, what do you say? Nothing! Just as I thought. Tell me something. Eadie Wilt. Is that your name?"

Eadie Wilt told her about her grandmother Alice, who looked after her husband's mother.

"Ah, that was your great-grandmother," said Charlotte, "If I understand correctly."

Eadie nodded.

"She was strong and stubborn and very heavy to lift into the bath."

Eadie Wilt's grandmother lived in Prahran and her old mother-in-law had the habit, when she was over ninety, of hauling her tusch on to the window sill and pissing out of the window.

Charlotte was excited by this not too distant origin that drew Eadie Wilt into the conspiracy of Jewdom with herself and Gertrude. Charlotte and Gertrude talked irritably together. They had been girls together in Berlin, before Auschwitz and Bergen-Belsen or Dachau and Brown Shirts or the Gestapo. Gertrude had photographs of them with blood-red lipstick, pencilled brows and Marcel waves.

"We Jewesses", said Gertrude, "always talk at cross purposes."

My beautiful Morma, thought Eadie Wilt, who was well and truly in love. With her Mongolian face, and Sophia Loren mouth, and Gertrude Stein haircut, this was how she looked to Eadie Wilt. She knitted beautiful suits for herself on the finest needles in dove-grey wool with jade inlay in the buttons.

Eadie Wilt met her when she was twelve. She was his mother, the boy with the turquoise eyes that paled and went transparent on hot days; the boy with the androgynous cardigans and feathery eyelashes and hair of yellow flame flowers, just as they turned orange and dropped to the ground.

When Gerald took Eadie Wilt to his mother's house, Gertrude was waiting for her. She had been waiting a long time. Since she had stood in the long queue in her boots and her yellow star, to abort her

daughters, she had been waiting for her. She cried
and told Eadie, "I killed my daughters."

She hugged and kissed and loved Eadie Wilt long
before her son did. Eadie Wilt was only twelve and
could turn away from no one who took her face
between their hands like this. Gertrude wrapped her
in her powerful arms and Eadie throbbed against her
strong neck, smelling of the skin balm that she used,
made by Mrs Fink in Block Arcade.

They went swimming at the city baths, Gertrude in
her heavy-skirted woollen bathers and Eadie Wilt in
her new flowery cottons that always got caught in her
bum crack. Gertrude breast-stroked noisily up and
down, and boys sniggered. When Eadie Wilt ran
away from home, she returned furtively to the street
to eat chicken soup with Morma. Her own misunder-
stood mother, ten houses away, did not know this.
Gerald took her to French films at the university on
Tuesday afternoons, and she noticed that he was so
lovely that he was stared at wherever he went. Eadie
dressed in Gertrude's 1940s dresses with hand pleat-
ing and stern white collars. Eadie and Gertrude
would go to the Block Arcade and buy skin balm
from Mrs Fink and eat city sandwiches. When
they went home, they would collect small hard pears
from the tree outside the blue kitchen, and lie on the
grass under the pear tree with bare legs, bold and
unladylike; Eadie Wilt peeling off her bohemian
black tights that Gertrude had bought for her at the
ballet shop.

When Gertrude died, Eadie Wilt was forty and only she could know that she loved Gertrude with a childhood's passion and mourned her with the deepest needs of an ancient girlhood grief.

When Eadie Wilt walked home, ten houses away from Anna Wesoloski and her daughter, Gertrude Friedman, she felt as if she was going to the wrong house with the wrong mother waiting for her.

"What is the matter?" asked her mother.

"Is something wrong?" asked her teachers.

She daydreamed, her mouth set in a dreadful scowl, and an air of fanaticism lit the unfocused eyes. Her strong and slender girl's body was acquainted with movement. She ran along, ever moving, light and quick on her feet, precise and excited.

To Anna Wesoloski, she was the girl down the street, the girl who came to visit and listen to the old stories of how it had been at the embroidery shop in Berlin. They had been such prosperous independent women of means then, until some *meshug* men had started talking of purification of the Fatherland. In the hall at Gertrude's house, there was a big heavy wooden box and inside was Anna Wesoloski's linen, a few choice pieces that Gertrude had managed to save, and take out of Germany. Gertrude had carried this box through the war and across several countries. When Eadie Wilt grew up, Gertrude gave her this box and Eadie kept it with her all her life. Her pillow slips had "Anna Wesoloski" embroidered on the corners in dark red cottons.

"Why do you waste your time gossiping down there?" asked her mother.

The oblique eloquent promise of "never getting nowhere" was a foolish thing but Eadie suddenly saw that her mother wanted her to cause an uproar, not with frivolous and trivial things but something large and gallant and helpful.

"Time is never wasted, Mum!" she offered. "Don't expect of me a legendary and impeccable future."

Paddy pursed her lips. She always got lost in Eadie's annoying maze of sentences. Wherever did she pick this up from, this tortuous way of explaining herself?

Eadie began to use Yiddish phrases that Anna Wesoloski had taught her, and it drove Paddy up the wall.

Anna's Box

Inside the wooden box where Anna Wesoloski's linen still remained, there were the remnants of her family, hidden at the bottom, old papers and photographs of perished generations.

She had owned an emboidery shop in Berlin, "Anna Wesoloski's Fine Linen". Walls of spools of fine yarns and catalogues of designs. Most women wanted their initials entwined and scrolled back then. Dark red was the dominating colour, or white against white. Pure cottons and the lustrous strong linen.

"You could not wash the *body* from this *linen*," said Anna Wesoloski.

The trunk had left Berlin with Gertrude. It had gone to Singapore where she had opened a guest-house. When they arrived in Australia after the war, they used it as a table in the internment camp. In Australia, the Jews were treated like undesirable aliens.

"In Germany, we were in the camps because we were Jews. In Australia, we were in other camps because we were German! Never mind," said Gertrude. "We were pleased to be alive."

Gertrude made herself a sunfrock from a blue

embroidered cloth from the box. Sometimes she used a pillowslip to tear up as bandages. She did not feel bad about this; the linen of Anna Wesoloski was serving a good purpose.

Anna Wesoloski had not wanted to leave Berlin. The Brown Shirts were delinquents, nothing more; nothing to get excited about. When they first appeared on the streets in groups, she pushed through them. This bustling old Jewish dowager disbanded them momentarily and they roared with laughter at her.

Things changed rapidly. That which you were laughed at for in January, you would be killed for in May.

Anna Wesoloski had no fear. Her world was the cloth before her, her head bent to the task, from seven in the morning till seven at night. She formed scrolls and letters and borders, buttonholes and eyelets. Her eyes were strong and she threaded the finest needles by instinct. She had no inkling that, within months, she would be fashioning yellow stars, and yellow stars only, for everyone she knew.

Gertrude's husband of that time was an intellectual, who was always in the cafe, talking politics.

"Talk, talk," said Anna, "and now he talks of leaving Germany and a good business."

One day, this husband, Werner was his name, received a notice to report to the administration office. He went there and did not return. They searched for him everywhere, and Gertrude and Anna went every day and sat on a bench at the administration office. A slow terror accelerated around them. They were told in clipped, threatening tones not to come back again, or they'd go missing too!

A woman who had always bought from Anna now came to the shop and handled the fabrics roughly. Anna gently took some lace slip covers from the matron who had been her customer for many years. She had dropped them on the ground and stood on them before asking for the price to be reduced. The women stood face to face, standing as they had many times, discussing an embroidery that the matron fancied. Without warning, with stupifying suddenness, the woman punched Anna with a fist, pink and knotted.

"*Jude bitch*!"

The whispered obscenity came from a repressed grimace and she looked as if she would burst into a panic of tears. Anna ducked, but the blow caught her eye and the cut bled on to the linen. Anna insisted that it would go no further than that. That night the windows were broken and the shop was boarded up. The glasscutter refused to cut a new glass, saying he was booked up for months.

Three months after Werner went missing, Gertrude received a telephone call.

"Hello?"

"Gertrude. It is me!"

The voice on the line was her husband's voice, but Gertrude was derailed from recent events. She could not know for sure if it was really him.

"I am in a labour camp. I may return home if you follow these instructions. Do these three things," he said.

There had been no reassurances or messages of endearment. She sat stunned. From the travel agent, she knew that Jews were leaving the country in droves. The only passage available was to Trinidad. She purchased three one-way tickets to Trinidad. Her mother was silent during these transactions. She sat in the back room, finishing her orders for blouses and chemises for the ballet school. When Gertrude had done the three things, she packed the trunk with linen and waited. The telephone rang again.

She was told by the voice of Werner to take the tickets to the administration building.

"I am not going to Trinidad," said Anna Wesoloski to her daughter. "I am going back to Poland, to my sisters. If there is trouble, I shall be well there."

The same young man who had threatened her before, stamped her papers and told her to go to a destination two miles beyond Berlin's city limits. Here, on the other side of the road, Gertrude found Werner. He had on a strange coat. It was not his.

"Who does this coat belong to?" questioned Gertrude, as he held her tightly. He smiled and kissed her with a new knowledge. He was young but he was a husband that always came home with a new knowledge. His beautiful red hair had been shorn, his fine-boned face was looking inquisitively up at her. The cuffs of his sleeves covered his hands and he slumped on the roadside. She tried to pull him up to her and he rose heavily like an animal who had decided to die. She folded back the cuffs of the coat and saw that his hands were swollen and the skin on the upper part of his hand was filled with pus. A small wounded moan seeped from her as she saw this. Something awakened in him and he gestured towards the car.

"Come! We have no time for this! We are the lucky ones."

A hint of his old impatient agility returned. They went home. There was a letter from Anna, a short letter. A good-bye letter. "I have gone to my sisters," it said. Sixteen weeks later, they were expecting to disembark in Trinidad but discovered that they had sailed instead to Singapore. They slept on the deck with hundreds of other confused, talkative people. The ship is sailing in circles, thought Gertrude. It didn't matter.

They took the box of Anna Wesoloski and began again. They opened a guesthouse in Singapore. They glassed in the verandah and filled it with giant cane chairs, where elderly Europeans sang songs and played cards, and listened to the war on the radio, and cried for home. No one knew yet of Auschwitz or Bergen-Belsen or Buchenwald. Anna Wesoloski was in a camp. The letters to her sister in Poland were not answered. Her sister was also in a camp, and no letters were delivered to that house anymore.

When Anna was on that terrible train that went on for weeks, she closed her eyes and thought up designs for new scroll work. She laid them out in her head and catalogued them.

The train stopped. She prepared for the worst. She realised that she was trapped in something unbelievable and she must live through it. All the people were stripped and divided, and two lines formed. She was put into the least desirable one, though she did not know it. They were told to move forward. A commandeering man barked at them.

"Move forward, seamstresses!"

Many who could, did not step forward. They were afraid to step from the crowd. They were in a catatonic trance of numbing fear. They could not yet formulate the simple and obvious idea that stepping out of the crowd could save their life.

Anna stepped forward, her hands clasped before her. Her head she held back as if she was fully dressed, a proud old woman, not arrogant, but erect. The man went from one to the other, impatient to make a choice.

"And you?" he barked as he came back to Anna Wesoloski.

"I am the proprietor of the finest embroidery establishment in Berlin," she said.

"The very finest," he said, a laugh in his bark.

"Without a doubt," she said, and so she was saved. She was put in the sorting shed for some time, going through piles of clothes taken from the people arriving twice daily at the camp. She knew that her sister and her sister's children had been killed. She felt a floating feeling in her head. Once she was hit with a rifle butt and realised that she did not feel pain, not pain as she remembered it.

She was taken to the inner compound, where a German officer lived with his wife and family. There was a fairy-story picket fence, a postage stamp of German folklore. Anna sat at a machine and made seven covers for feather beds. They were monogrammed and scrolled in six colours.

She tried all the designs that she had made up on the train. She embroidered the officer's uniforms and underwear, just as she had sewn yellow stars on the overcoats of her neighbours in Berlin.

In the afternoons, the German wife, Tineka, had afternoon tea with the other officers' wives.

"These are designs for my new slip covers," she would say, as she passed around Anna's immaculate drawings done that afternoon at the table in the basement. "What do you think?"

"But who will do the needlework?" they asked, and the woman smiled and cut into the poppyseed cake. She wanted to keep Anna her secret for as long as she could.

Every day Anna was called to the picket fence to work at the white linen. She had to be clean. She now was scrubbed raw with a harsh washing compound and dressed in a white cotton house dress while she worked at the fine lace and handkerchief edging for small gifts for the other wives. At night she returned to the barracks, to the grim faces of the other women.

She was searched, but she always had something stitched into the hem of her dress, a reminder of life outside, a life they would return to: an almond biscuit or a small piece of cheese that they shared and were afraid that everyone could smell; some hard jubes that you could only buy in Berlin, that they sucked on all night. All the women in Anna's row died, but Anna kept on, due to her needlework. When someone died, her eyes were red at work, and Tineka, the German wife, would be curious.

"What's the matter with you?" Tineka would ask. Anna Wesoloski did not say that her friends had been slaughtered. She did not say that one had been kicked so hard in the head that her eye had popped from its socket. She did not say that she knew this woman from home and that she had been known for her exceptional blue eyes that made you think of heaven. She did not look up, but mumbled, "I am thinking of home."

The woman nodded. This was acceptable. She herself had often cried for home. She knew that, despite the "Fatherland", all women were the same under the skin.

One day, Anna was sent by Tineka on an errand. She was sent with a package for Tineka's husband. It was unfamiliar territory, and she walked warily. She came around the main wooden barracks and stopped. Unexpectedly, a child stood there sobbing, her feet and legs splattered with blood. A uniformed man stood to the left of Anna. He was turned towards the child and spoke to another officer.

"You can see she's ripe," he giggled, spluttering in a crazy sort of mirth. Anna could see now that it was Tineka's husband and his friend from behind the picket fence. The package that she held was a large pocket handkerchief which she herself had embroidered. It was extremely special. It had the man's full name, entwined in relief with the swastika emblem and the face of Hitler behind the lettering. She had been given a photograph of the Führer, which she had reduced to light and shade and embroidered in several tones of grey. Tineka had arranged that her husband give this birthday present to his friend, Heinrich, on his departure from the camp that afternoon. It had not been completed in the morning, so Tineka had sent the package with Anna. These errands could mean instant death for Anna but she had no choice but to follow Tineka's orders. The handkerchief was plump and white beneath its thin covering of transparent tissue, with one strand of black ribbon tying it together. You could see the embroidery quite clearly through the paper. The man lifted the hem of the child's dress with the barrel of his gun. Her face streamed with tears. She could have been eleven, but the evidence of menstruation made it likely that she was older. She was wearing a pair of old men's underpants. He told her to take them off and wipe her face. It was the moment that Anna decided was her courageous moment. She knew it would come, she had saved herself for it as a woman once did for marriage. She took two strong steps forward. All attention was suddenly on her. She shook the large handkerchief free by pulling at the velvet ribbon. The handkerchief was startling. White and brilliant and clever. The two men focused on it immediately, saw what it was! Hitler's face, a masterpiece in tonal contrast and the bold lettering, "Heinrich," against it in red. Anna held it aloft for some seconds before she quickly moved to the girl and wiped her face. The men were immobile until she began to move the girl away from them. One came quickly, she did not see which one, she saw the gun raised and his outline against a grey sky. As she looked up, he brought the gun down into her face. Heinrich was keen to finish her off, especially when he saw his handkerchief so messed up with the Jew's blood. "No. No! This is Tineka's woman," said the husband, and they made the girl drag her back to barracks and hose her down. Anna was pleased that she had lived through her moment of courage.

"It may be my only one," she told the girl. Anna's nose was broken and she lost two teeth; she looked lopsided when she smiled. She patted her nose and thought, It's still a Jew's nose." She was once again called to the picket fence. Tineka grew irrational if she did not see her every day.

Anna began a tablecloth appliquéd with cherries, with napkins to match, and she had lengthy conversations with Tineka. They drew up lists of "things" to make and sometimes the German woman thought Anna was her dead mother and did not want her to go "back". She would keep her there until the husband came in and nodded Anna toward the door. He would shake his head at the new dress his Tini had dressed the ugly old Jew in. It was why he loved her, he said. She was a soft thing, goodness all through.

When Anna was very, very old and had come through all this, had come to Melbourne, Australia, she would sometimes say things that disturbed people.

"Even in concentration camp, I always had a pretty dress."

Anyone who heard this and did not know her story thought this a queer senile thing to say, but Eadie Wilt knew the story, the missing links. She understood why Anna Wesoloski still cried.

Eadie Wilt was an only child. She was sad about that. Brother was a big word for her and Sister, born of the same mother and father. But she laughed until her ears went red when Anna chased Gerald under the bed. She told Anna of her great-grandmother who pissed out of the window in Prahran and the butcher who told her she did it because she was an old Jew.

"I am an old Jew and I don't piss out of the window," said Anna. "Perhaps I am not old enough."

"I think a lot about the people from those days," said Anna to Eadie Wilt.

"Poor soft Tineka, the German wife, was worse off than any of us." Eadie stayed silent. She couldn't see the truth in that.

"When we were liberated, we just walked out of the camp with no direction. I looked over there towards the picket fence. I wanted to see her one more time. It was deserted. Some said she had suicided."

Anna took a long deep breath and hugged Eadie Wilt into her cardigan before she continued.

"When I looked into her eyes, and I was told never to do that, she let me look at her, she looked back, not as a stranger. Behind that pale wide forehead was a very simple will, not ever to destruct. Her will was dictated by a formula confined to her table and the house she presided over. She liked to see me eat the same bread that she ate. She wanted to learn to make button-holes but feared that she would never master it. "If it's worth doing, it's worth doing badly," I told her. "Badly can always be made better.""

"Otto," Tineka would sigh, when her husband came in, and she took his cruel hands in hers and tried to purify him and play the game of marriage. But the strange smells on him made her shiver. Otto told her that she must never go outside the picket fence.

"I shall be so glad when this embarrassment is out of the way," he told her to explain her confinement. She had heard the screaming of children.

"It is only a dream. Have some more tea. Here, there is no room for such feelings. Don't be afraid, you are a good wife. Don't forget our secret smile."

He feared, however, that her spring had snapped.

"Poor Tineka thinks that old Jew is her own mother," he thought. She was always coming towards him and laying her hands on his shoulders to look squarely into his eyes. This made him more afraid than anything the war had brought him.

Once she went through the picket fence and met him at the barracks gate. He was livid, and slapped her. She walked back to the house, through the mud and blood, in her white dress. He drew her back through the picket fence. She did not resist as he pulled her along by the wrist.

"Murderers are not murderers twenty-four hours a day," she said to him. Tineka was searching for a reason, to devise a way to take her away from all of this.

She wanted to go outside, beyond the electric fences. She told me that she would never in her life go out of the picket fence again. Then she bit her lip and grew formal.

"Otto says I give you too many privileges; that you should eat what others eat and wear the clothes that others wear."

Tineka told him that she would eat rotten bread too and he laughed his hidden laugh.

"We will soon be away," he told her, "and there will be snow on the mountains when we go home, ice on the streams." Tineka thought how his laugh had gone sour and squeezed tight, like a frightful password. "He is one of them," she thought. "Blemished all through. I could shoot him in his sleep, take careful aim."

But it was too high a price too pay. So she allowed herself to be a little mad.

"Good afternoon, darling. Is death made of metal?" she asked coquetishly. "Are the people wailing out there? Come in."

Her husband kissed her on the cheek and took her to bed. He knew she was damning him.

Later when Anna saw the *Life* magazine photographs of German soldiers goose-stepping, she tried to find Otto or Heinrich, who drank cognac on the granite steps and beat old women down night after night and laughed behind the pergola, as Tineka leaned over the balustrade of the house behind the picket fence. The air smelled foul at certain times of the day. Heinrich with his bourgeois moustache sang seriously his Fatherland songs. He made children stand for hours in the ice at night until loathsome purple blotches spread along their legs. Their leg muscles and chest muscles and mouth muscles cramped and they sank down while he was at home, behind the picket fence.

"Tineka must be dead," decided Anna Wesoloski.

Eadie Wilt walked home, ten houses away from Anna Wesolsoski who lived with her daughter Gertrude, who had recently married the older brother from the smallgoods business in Glenhuntly Road. Towards the end of Eadie's childhood, though no one can say for sure when something ends or something else begins, Eadie Wilt met her second family. They had a smallgoods business with a fleet of vans that ran around town delivering their product. They were very distinctive vans, painted a special shade of pale green with a giant cut salami painted on the side panels in tones of pink and red.

If Anna Wesoloski's stories made her feel burdened, Eadie would always be light-hearted when she saw Gerald drivng one of these vans with the salami on its side. He had not been driving for long and Eadie was not allowed to go in the car with him. Until she had gone to Gertrude's house, she wrote in her marbled notebook, of not belonging to the earth.

One day, she went to Gertrude's, and Anna Wesoloski was dead and Gertrude had candles burning in the blue kitchen.

Cry Yourself Blind

Eadie Wilt left her mother's house at a very early, young age. Eadie's sudden adjustment to runaway status caused them both, with quivering-lipped inevitability, to cry themselves blind. Eadie's leaving was a spontaneous thing. A rumble had been caused in Eadie, the day before the primal event, by an incident with her father, Frankie Wilt. Paddy on this day was wearing a cream silk shirt and a pair of tailored velvet hipsters that reduced her tiny frame to matchstick proportions. She was having one of those wild-eyed conversations with her gawky kid about heart-breaking issues of life and death that mothers and daughters should not get into. They continued with this discussion until Frankie Wilt beeped his horn at the front fence, to pick Eadie up. Paddy, poised like a skinny reptile in the front door, felt lonely. It was a period of despair. Somewhere deep, she wanted to go with her devilish urchin and her childhood love, Frankie Wilt, to wherever they went on these afternoon excursions. As Eadie slouched into the car, she hissed, "What a bitch." This was the first time she had ever tried this approach and Frankie slung the Holden into reverse and glared at her. It got the afternoon off to a very bad start. This collision with her father was rare and blatant.

"Don't speak of her like that," he said laconically. He could trace early ecstasy to Paddy and he never escaped the teetering landscapes of his boyhood paradise. Under duress, he might admit that she was not real smooth to live with. On the other hand, Paddy was archly brutal in her packaging of him. Eadie did not understand his politeness.

They made their way very slowly down the street. Frankie drove dangerously slow. He still had chronic breathing problems and physically he was short-changed by his ruthlessly damaged body. He was spectrally thin, with an endearing gentle drawl and an easy acceptance of a world that he might have to leave at any time. He felt strong to Eadie, free and bright, and she took notice of everything he said. He did not say much usually. It was too much effort. Every now and then, he summoned up a flash of energy and expressed it with such clear-eyed and radical physical consequence that lesser human contact was usurped and mowed down by this dazzling rapturous flicker of strong blind strength.

This hot gleaming day bounced around in her memory, an afternoon when she expected every kind of magic. They approached the end of the street, the heat pounding down on the bonnet of the Holden. Ahead of them was the bottle-o. His horse and cart was loaded up with bottles he had collected from the houses. Several people were shovelling up horse manure for their garden. Frankie Wilt kept the motor running and waited behind the cart.

"You could not get past in a month of Sundays," said Frankie Wilt, who was squinting at the situation, putting two and two together. The horse was old, the cart was overloaded, the wheels were not turning, the horse was being feverishly urged to pull. The back wheels seemed to be sinking into melting asphalt. The sun pelted down, extra hot. Out came the whip, with a resigned smile from the bottleman; a jolting shock as the crack ripped the polite afternoon. The horse's flanks quivered and trembled. He went down in a slow sinking spread of legs. Frankie Wilt, the unknown quantity, did not miss a beat. He was out there, crushing back the man. The mossy toothed bottle-o flashed his dental metal in a chain of nervous smile grimaces. Frankie had unstrapped the horse and the cart dropped with smart destructive intelligence that was hard to ignore. A crowd gathered. Broken bottles filled the road and gutters. The renegade and his partner in crime, Eadie, stood facing the neighbour-hood people, not especially perturbed or impressed by the heroic prospects of the afternoon. The Animal Protection people were called and they took the horse off to an old horse paddock somewhere. The bottle-o sat in the gutter, hopelessly, insanely angst-ridden. People offered him jobs. In a neighbourhood as dense-ly Jewish as Caulfield was becoming, this was to be expected. The prospect of failure was not alienating, necessarily, not in this new, hybrid Australia.

As Eadie and Frankie drove off, she looked at her father who was winding down from the monumental "sexy, dangerous and alive" exultation of the encounter. She had unwittingly collaborated crudely with the action. It was addictive stuff, standing up for things. Radical intervention, he called it. The bastard child of profound and helpful thought. An axis that changed imaginings, the idea of an alternative world, into movement, that changed the facts. Or did it? Anyway, that was the best thing that happened on their outing that afternoon because Frankie Wilt was too fucked-up to manage any more activity. They parked down on the water and watched the waves transcending the physical world of bodgies gathering on the pier; the tough, colloquial language was abstracted by the breaking of the waves. The adrenalin rush of their earlier adventure was all but forgotten by the endless lawless presence of the foaming surf.

The next day, the incident was still provoking her imagination. For some reason, Paddy ran at Eadie with her little fists blazing and Eadie stood firm.

"I'm tired of this, Mum," she said.

A great crack on the fault line of her heart made her shudder. Paddy fell back like a crushed canary hitting a brick wall. Eadie walked to the front door in a march, turned left out into the street, and didn't stop until she came to the house of the man who had the battered removal van. With his help, Eadie left home, even though she wasn't sure how to go about it. Paddy did not try to stop her daughter in any real way. She knew that something was changing drastically and irreversibly.

"I think that what we are now is on its way out," Eadie told her as she bundled her ragged dresses into a teabox with all her artworks and childhood keepsakes. Though she had seen her father the day before, she did not know exactly where he lived. Sometimes he had taken her to his abode of the moment. It could be a caravan on a beach or a bungalow in a suburban ghetto or a hut in a cold forest. She had been to his present address without ever knowing the street name or number. Off she went, in the rattling old removal truck with a disoriented-looking bloke who collaborated with a strange and beautiful deafness. Responding to the textures of the day, the directions of her speech keyed into contact with the telepresence of his understanding. Though she cried herself blind and the light burned her already scorched eyes, she found herself some hours later, on the doorstep of her father. She had run away from home, and Paddy cried, back there, knowing that they'd missed their chance.

The guess-what surprise of the afternoon was that Frankie Wilt, without telling anyone, had recently married again. The new wife took one look at the big cheeky girl on the threshhold and shook her head. It was a mutant household. Frankie Wilt owned several unruly dogs who raced around the house inside and out, tearing up things from the clothesline, or anything, really. Neither passive nor well-trained, they caused havoc. The house had been a normal estate house when Frankie moved in, but now it was a nightmarish vision. He had made stone pools around the house and planted willow trees beside these limpid, stagnant waterways. The roots of the willow trees in their thirsty search for more and more water had grown towards the sewerage system, and lifted and corroded the foundations of the house. Whole rooms leaned or sank at strange angles, as if the house was about to be wrenched from the ground and thrown into planetary orbit.

As Frankie's health deteriorated, he spat blood and lost his breath, so he sat in one place and made sculptures of horses on the walls of the house in plaster. He painted them, and moved his chair only when he had used up wall space. There were clothes-lines across all of the rooms, that crossed each other. They were low down, so Frankie could reach them. They had drawings and bills and pictures out of newspapers all pegged across the room like a chaotic sci-fi washday. Needless to say, Eadie did not stay with her father. She moved on quickly to Grandma Alice's house, vacillating between insight and ignorance in the same breath. She realised with humility that leaving home was full of contradictions. With a brief flash of sensitivity, she knew that her natural charm was not going to be enough soundtrack to her life. She couldn't see many ways out. She was not the little adored grandchild anymore. She was "big trouble". She missed Morma and the street, and she even missed Paddy.

She realised that she was uninformed about the hilarious and often humourless conditions of life. She would not see her mother again for a very long time, but when she did, she had by then found her secret adoring. This was the biggest problem later in life, because Paddy showed a thorny outrage to the notion of being adored.

The Inheritance

When Eadie Wilt was older, having her time, if life
went sour, she would close her eyes and see them all,
the whole mongrel lot of them. Thirty-odd handsome
women in open-necked shirts, polka dots and plaids
and stockmen's trousers and boots shined to the hilt.
Except, of course, the brat, Eadie Wilt!

"You can't ride a horse in a frock," yelled the aunties, but Eadie liked her legs bare and the wind lifting
her skirt up around her ears. "We can see your bum,"
they chorused, "and you look like a bold cheeky girl."
They galloped after the runt of a girl, flying and puffing until the horses came to a standstill and the women
lay ruffled and tousled on the grass, the great roaring
sky grinning down on them. Siddy Church let her cat,
Rufus, out of her saddlebag and Willy Howe sucked
on her pipe, while old Mantel looked for mushrooms
and ate all the boiled eggs from the picnic. Eadie Wilt,
when she was older, could lie in any garden and
remember the back wall where her grandmother
thinned the carrots. Eadie would fall asleep in the old
wheelbarrow, and Siddy would wheel it inside and
leave her in the kitchen beside the stove, still sleeping.
Later, when Siddy lived in the suburbs and was close to

the end, Eadie would visit and lie once more in the old barrow watching her grandmother filling a basket with lemons for her to take home. It was the only harvesting left to her she said, and remarked, distractedly, that the wheelbarrow would outlive them all.

Eadie forgot all about this wheelbarrow until the day her auntie rang and asked to meet her on the Punt Road bridge. Eadie arrived early and leaned over the railing, staring at the water. Streams of cars roared by. She could hardly hear herself think. When she looked up, the old woman was ploughing towards her, pushing Siddy's bloody wheelbarrow. It looked strange against the traffic.

"This is what Siddy wanted you to have," she said with a pecking kiss, trying to keep on the footpath with the giant wheelbarrow. In the wheelbarrow was Siddy Church's big old handbag with the pearl-handled derringer and numerous hankies, tied in a knot, holding as-yet-undiscovered treasures. It was a curious collection of jewellery. Sapphires bundled in with pink glass rings from cornflakes packets, promotional giveaways from the 1950s. There was a wad of two-dollar notes. These were for Eadie, for what Siddy had calculated would be her lifetime. One a week, continuing the habit already secured. Soon after, two dollar notes were recalled and a coin was introduced to replace them. Eadie changed them at the bank and filled the big black handbag with coins. They made the bag very heavy. Siddy Church had estimated a very long life for her grand-daughter.

Earthly Cares Spilling

When the coherence of childhood ended, Eadie Wilt stopped writing in her word-book. She plunged fragilely into the unmerciful years when nasty falls and wild nomadic flights transformed forever her shimmer of childhood radiance.

The sacred reassurances of Siddy Church held fast through the sprawling ragged years; the tough times that knocked Eadie Wilt on her tusch. "Breathe and live," she told herself when exhaustion touched her solidly. She waited for her great and wonderful life even while being right in the middle of it. She twisted and shuddered at every new implausible dilemma; trembled at the audacity, the ludicrous depths of sadness, the sudden conglomeration of subversive agenda that entered her life. The incandescent delights of unforeseen pursuits. The mystic erotic nomadic life, earthly cares, spilling, seeping.

Later, when she looked back, the comings and goings fell in on each other. She went to art school and sat next to a snowy-haired girl called Sandra. Her friend Gerald Anthony Hartwig went to Tunisia and Turkey, and she went to the beach with the bathing beauty. On the beach she met "the Americans". She was about to turn fourteen. In certain places, no one asked her age; in others, everyone did. The Americans were dancers and they had come to Australia with *West Side Story*. One short black man in cowboy boots and elastic shorts, called Joe Joe, took her along Fitzroy Street, past Leo's, to a door with a staircase into a darkened nightclub. It was hot outside. They were salty with sand on their feet. The dark cool place smelt smoky and was lit by a giant fish tank. A thin stream of water behind thick glass cut the room in two.

He sucked her ears and ran his salty tongue over her hot young face. She acted coyly virginal because she was. He told her that they were auditioning for understudies for the show and that he could teach her a simple choreography that would make her look like a trained dancer.

"You'll get the job," he told her, "because you look like a Puerto Rican Lolita."

All afternoon, she learnt steps with big excitement from Joe Joe.

"What is this place?" she asked.

"This is Birdland," he said with a one-two-three drop-kick-turn. Next day, he took her to the audition. They did not ask her age.

"That's the one," said the director, "She looks like a Puerto Rican Lolita."

Eadie Wilt went interstate with the show, but did not dance one night on stage. Instead she practised her one-two-three drop-kick-turn in places like Birdland.

She started art school while Gerald Hartwig was in Nepal, and ate regularly with Morma and Walter Friedman. It did not occur to her that they might not have loved her. She had no difficulties with the ambiguities of feelings. She loved them. There was no risk. She moved in with her Grandma Alice, the one with the mother-in-law who pissed out of the window. She lived a wild life, but her grandmother was a rare one who did not see things. She climbed in bed beside her, just moments before she woke to get ready for work in the knitting factory. Her grandmother had worked for thirty-five years throughout her entire married life, and now that she was a widow, she saw no reason to stop; she had no superannuation. Her wage would cease the day she stopped working.

To ease her guilt at being bad, Eadie polished the house. All the floors and the sideboards. She walked the streets, hand-picking the best flowers she could find, and she made dinner. Her grandmother could smell it when she came in, and she loved Eadie Wilt. When Eadie went to art school at Caulfield Technical School, she fell for Sandra, with the white hair that hung to her waist. Sandra told Eadie, "I'm going to be the highest-paid woman artist in Australia." They drew each other naked, and Eadie brushed the mermaid hair.

Together, they drew designs for toothpaste boxes in Advertising and shadowed cubes for Nature and Object.

Eadie Wilt also did an extra, English Literature.

One day Eadie was standing in Fitzroy Street. She no

longer looked like the Puerto Rican Lolita, she was into her black widow spider phase. She stood on the street with Joe Joe, and a girl called Mercedes Ellington, and several poets and poets' friends, when Gerald drove by in an Austin Seven motor car. He shrieked and waved, but did not stop. Eadie Wilt was delirious and realised that she had not seen Morma for months.

"My lovely friend is home," she said.

It is 1998. Siddy Church is dead. Paddy Wilt died not long after her first love, Frankie. Anna Wesoloski's box is under the stairs at Eadie's house. Gertrude's house with the blue kitchen has been pulled down, and the tree with the small hard pears is gone. Even Gerald Anthony Hartwig is dead. He was the first one to die of all the ones that Eadie loved best. The eager sensuous beauty appeared once more in his daughter and grand-daughter. All the grandmothers and grand-fathers are gone, and little Eadie Wilt is the oldest now.

I sit in my garden in the early summer freshness of small yellow climbing roses and pale pink geraniums. The tall grass has buttercups, and washing hangs in a long line under the trees. A double blue gate at the bottom of the garden is where your old wheelbarrow stands.

The wind lifts and sighs. My heart exhausts itself with longing.

Imago
Francesca Rendle-Short

Imago is a story of love and obsession, of seductions
and transformations. The threading together
of skins, of bodies.
Award-winning writer Francesca Rendle-Short
writes with poetic ease, her sensual language rich
with metaphor and symbol.

ISBN 1-875559-36-1

Wee Girls
edited by Lizz Murphy

Women, writing from an Irish perspective in
Australia, Ireland, England, America, Canada and
New Zealand.

A moving and often amusing collection of fiction,
poetry and autobiography by
top-selling and award-winning writers.

Tales of blood and bloodlines – Irish grandmothers,
ma's and da's, the Famine and The Troubles.
Whatever the form, there are the stories, the music,
the whispering dreams and the voices that
ache to be heard.

Ancient history, myth and legend are balanced
with the fragility and tenuousness of contemporary
society, peace and exile.

There is a wildness and daring in these voices. They
call up legions out of the sea and set fires alight.
They hang out over garden fences, move restlessly,
are dotey, beaming, weeping, powerful.

ISBN 1-875559-51-5

Safe Houses
Rose Zwi

Against the background of the escalating violence of
South Africa in the 80s, *Safe Houses* tells the
story of three families – black and Jewish – who are
inextricably bound by love and hate,
hope and betrayal.
Winner of the Human Rights Award for Fiction.

ISBN 1-875559-21-3

Another Year in Africa
Rose Zwi

They came from the shtetl to a new land, to a new
life. Another year in Africa, they said, another year
in exile.

Award-winning author Rose Zwi evokes with
tenderness, the 1930s and 40s. A loss of innocence
and the stirrings of apartheid.
Winner of the Olive Schreiner Award.

ISBN 1-875559-42-6

If you would like to know more about Spinifex
Press, write for a free catalogue or visit
our home page.

SPINIFEX PRESS
PO Box 212, North Melbourne,
Victoria 3051, Australia
http://www.publishaust.net.au/~spinifex